PRAISE FOR THE REVEREND ANNABELLE DIXON COZY MYSTERY SERIES

"Absolutely wonderful!!"
"Descriptions of even the most commonplace are beautiful."
"The best Annabelle book you've done."
"Another winner. Loved it. Can't wait for the next one."
"I couldn't put it down!"
"Best book yet, Alison. I'm not kidding. You did a heck of a job."
"I read it that night, and it was GREAT!"
"Grab it and read it, my friends."
"A real page turner and a perfect cozy mystery."
"As a former village vicar this ticks the box for me."
"I enjoyed this book from the first line to the last page."
"Annabelle, with her great intuition, caring personality, yet imperfect judgement, is a wonderful main character."
"It's fun to grab a cup of tea and pretend I'm sitting in the vicarage discussing the latest mysteries with Annabelle whilst she polishes off the last of the cupcakes."
"Great book - love Reverend Annabelle Dixon and can't wait to read more of her books."
"Annabelle reminds me of Agatha Christie's Miss Marple."

"A perfect weekend read."
"Terrific cozy mystery!"
"A wonderful read, delightful characters and if that's not enough the sinfully delicious recipes will have you coming back for more."
"Love the characters, the locations and the plots get twistier with each book."
"My own pastoral career has been pretty exciting, but I confess Annabelle has me beat!"
"This new book rocks."
"Writer has such an imagination!"
"Believable and quirky characters make it fun."
"This cozy series is a riot!"

WITCHES AT THE WEDDING

BOOKS IN THE REVEREND ANNABELLE DIXON SERIES

Chaos in Cambridge (Prequel)

Death at the Café

Murder at the Mansion

Body in the Woods

Grave in the Garage

Horror in the Highlands

Killer at the Cult

Fireworks in France

Witches at the Wedding

COLLECTIONS

Books 1-4

Death at the Café

Murder at the Mansion

Body in the Woods

Grave in the Garage

Books 5-7

Horror in the Highlands

Killer at the Cult

Fireworks in France

WITCHES AT THE WEDDING

ALISON GOLDEN

JAMIE VOUGEOT

The characters and events portrayed in this book are fictitious. Any similarity to real persons, living or dead is coincidental and not intended by the author.
Text copyright © 2022 Alison Golden
All rights reserved.

No part of this book may be reproduced, stored in a retrieval system, or transmitted in any form or by any means, electronic, mechanical, photocopying, recording, or otherwise, without express written permission of the publisher.

Published by Mesa Verde Publishing
P.O. Box 1002
San Carlos, CA 94070

ISBN: 979-8437154366

"People will forget what you said, people will forget what you did, but people will never forget how you made them feel."
- Maya Angelou -

"Your emails seem to come on days when I need to read them because they are so upbeat."
- Linda W -

For a limited time, you can get the first books in each of my series - *Chaos in Cambridge, Hunted* (exclusively for subscribers - not available anywhere else), *The Case of the Screaming Beauty,* and *Mardi Gras Madness* - plus updates about new releases, promotions, and other Insider exclusives, by signing up for my mailing list at:

https://www.alisongolden.com/annabelle

CHAPTER ONE

"**THREE DAYS!**" PHILIPPA muttered to herself as she plucked a sheet from the washing line and tossed it into the basket beside her. "Only three days left! And she's barely prepared anything!"

Above the rippling, rustling clothes, a pale morning sun cast a gentle glow across Annabelle's cottage. It promised a warm April day. A mild breeze stirred into motion the flowers and shrubs in the pretty cottage garden.

Biscuit, Annabelle's ginger tabby, stalked along the small brick wall that separated the cottage from the fields beyond. She plopped herself down in a sunny spot on top of the wall and stretched out, licking her paws as Magic, Annabelle's dog, scampered around Philippa's feet. The dog was boisterous but wise enough not to get too close to the basket of washing. He knew from experience that Philippa would shoo him away and spoil his fun.

"Does she think the wedding will organise itself?" Philippa picked off the pegs pinning one of Annabelle's clerical undergarments to the washing line and roughly tangled it into a ball. She'd iron it later. Raising her face to the clear blue sky, she closed her eyes, feeling the sun's warmth penetrating her eyelids. "Oh, God, give me strength. I know she's a vicar—one of yours—but she's driving me to distraction. Help me make her see sense."

Philippa continued to toss clothes into the basket, and when the line was empty, Magic still leaping around her, she hoisted the basket onto her hip and stomped towards the cottage. Combining a deft nudge of her toe with the pirouetting skill of a ballerina, Philippa pushed the door open and sidestepped into the cottage, shutting the door with a precisely judged flick of her heel.

"Morning, Philippa," Annabelle said, emerging from the kitchen in a pink bathrobe. She rubbed her wet hair with a towel.

"Morning, Reverend," Philippa said, swallowing her frustration and trapping her thoughts in her mind where they continued to swirl like bees in a jar. She put the basket down beside the ironing board with a bang and shook out a fitted clerical shirt with three-quarter-length sleeves. She whipped it like a sail in a storm. Annabelle took a step back in alarm.

"Goodness, Philippa, you're sharp this morning. Anyone would think you were angry about something." Philippa shook the shirt some more. Annabelle frowned. She liked that shirt. She considered her wrists one of her best features.

Philippa picked up the iron, avoiding Annabelle's gaze. "Have you given any thought to savouries for the reception yet? Sausage rolls or Cornish pasties? We've got plenty of sweets planned." Philippa looked at Annabelle and raised one eyebrow. "But we need to have something for those with different tastes."

Annabelle laughed easily as she moved to the kitchen

counter. "Gosh, no!" she said. "I've just woken up. The only thought on my mind right now is breakfast." It was Philippa's turn to frown, but Annabelle was too busy pouring herself a cup of tea and placing a hot slice of toast on a plate to notice.

On the kitchen table were a host of papers. Annabelle walked over and set her breakfast down. Philippa's frown morphed into wide-eyed horror. Annabelle had placed her tea and toast directly on top of the wedding guest list and meticulous, handwritten notes that Philippa had spent hours poring over. She had laid them on the table for the vicar's inspection.

But it was what Annabelle did next that made Philippa's blood pressure skyrocket. Instead of noticing Philippa's hard work, making a comment, or even perhaps perusing the list of RSVPs, Annabelle blithely grabbed the morning newspaper. She spread it across Philippa's papers before taking a big bite of her toast and leant over to read the headlines!

Philippa's eyes shrunk, her bloodless lips twisted, and her lower jaw was set askew. She became almost unrecognisable. "Unbelievable!" she muttered.

"What's that?" Annabelle said, not looking up as she turned the front page. Philippa gawped at her, incredulous. She involuntarily twitched when Annabelle laughed out loud at something she was reading. The more Annabelle relaxed, the more Philippa's anxiety and frustration grew. She was boiling.

This was too much. Beyond the pale. Philippa opened her mouth, ready to unleash all her irritation, to transgress the boundaries of politeness in a final attempt to shake the vicar into some semblance of sanity with respect to her wedding preparations. But before Philippa could find the words, the morning silence was broken by the sharp tring of the telephone.

"Would you mind getting that, Philippa?" Annabelle mumbled through a mouthful of toast. When Philippa didn't move, Annabelle raised her eyes from her newspaper to gaze at her. "Please."

Philippa clenched her fists, breathed heavily through her nose, and stomped to the telephone. After a brief exchange, she returned to the kitchen. "That was Father John. He's on his way and says he should be here in an hour or two. He says he's looking forward to getting you married."

Annabelle's eyes lit up. "Oh, wonderful! He's rather early though, isn't he? We don't need him until the wedding rehearsal. That isn't until Friday evening."

"Early?" Philippa gasped, her voice high and breathless. Anger coursed through her body, tension that had been increasing for days. "Annabelle," she said, forcing herself to speak calmly. "There's just three more days left to prepare for your wedding. Three days."

Annabelle looked up from her newspaper. She continued to chew on a piece of toast, but her jaw slowed as she considered what Philippa had said. Eventually, she replied. "Yes. I suppose you're right. Do you think Father John will be bored staying so long?"

Philippa squeezed her eyes so tight she saw stars. Her inability to convey the immense gravity of the wedding situation to Annabelle caused her consternation the like of which she hadn't felt since Biscuit brought home a dead rat and dropped it into her cake mix when she wasn't looking.

"Vicar!" Philippa said, marching to Annabelle's side. She leant over to fold the newspaper. "You have three days to coordinate dozens of people so that your wedding occurs without mishap. Three days to ensure your marriage follows the correct protocol of ceremony, reception, and honeymoon, preferably in that order. Three days to ensure all the visitors, guests, and well-wishers, of which there are many, have places to stay, are adequately fed and entertained, and also leave on time, so they don't stay here forever. Three days to finalise the perfect dress, the perfect music, the perfect food, and the perfect vows. Three days to show your future husband what a prize of a bride he has won. Three days to plan and execute the biggest event of your life!"

CHAPTER TWO

ANNABELLE STARED. PHILIPPA pulled Annabelle's plate away and brushed crumbs from the plans she had laid out on the table. She tried to ignore the grease spot that now sullied the carefully written lists into which she had expended so much energy. "Here. I have laid out everything that needs to be done. I've organised by deadline, colour-coded by category, and marked everything that has yet to be completed with a star, which is virtually every item. See?"

"You make it sound like a military operation!" Annabelle quipped, still loudly munching away.

"Oh no!" Philippa corrected her, snatching the toast from Annabelle's hand. "It's far more important than that! They don't take photos that you'll look at forever during military operations! You are our vicar, um, Vicar, and a person of standing around these parts. Your wedding will be talked about for years to come. It would be terrible if it were talked about for all the wrong reasons."

Annabelle chuckled and brushed her hands together. Crumbs sprinkled across the plans. Philippa made another attempt to sweep them away. "Good lord, Philippa," Annabelle said. "You're making a mountain out of a molehill. You're making a five-tier wedding cake out of a simple sandwich sponge!"

"I am NOT, Vicar! Enough jokes!" Philippa said. She marched to the other side of the table, glaring at Annabelle as she leant forwards, her palms flat on the tabletop. "When are you going to take this wedding seriously? At this rate you'll be married in the garden in front of the dogs and the cat wearing that bathrobe!"

"That sounds rather appealing, actually." Annabelle smiled, conjuring up the vision in her mind's eye before cutting herself short, noticing, finally, the church secretary's devastating scowl. "Look, Philippa, I keep telling you, it only has to be a simple wedding. I'm not a celebrity or royalty. I don't need my wedding to become some overelaborate, glamorous extravaganza—in fact, I'd much prefer it wasn't."

"You'll be lucky to get married at all at this rate!" Philippa exclaimed. "Like it or not, you're an integral member of our community, and there are a lot of people who have been anticipating your wedding for years. The whole village is so excited! Lord knows we've been waiting long enough!"

"Philippa!" Annabelle cried. "How rude!"

Philippa looked away, her expression mulish. "I'm sorry, Annabelle . . . But you've pushed me to this point," she said, only a little more calmly. "Now, I understand that you're the bride, and this is your special day. I'm willing to do everything I can to make your wedding wonderful—I will work night and day to get it right—but I can't do it all by myself, and I can't do it if I don't know what you want!"

Annabelle sighed and cast her eyes over the notes on the

table. There were lists of names and their assigned duties, times and schedules next to tasks and assignments, schematics of both the church and the reception marquee with numbers and letters scrawled in tiny script. "Gosh, Philippa, these look like battle plans for the invasion of a small country." She peered at the lists, scrutinising them one by one.

"That's because this is the invasion of a small country. Your wedding is invading normal life in this village for one day."

"I understand," Annabelle said, "and I appreciate how much you're doing for me. But I did say that I wanted a small, cosy wedding with only a few people present. That's all. I'll let love and the good Lord account for the rest."

Philippa pulled back a chair and dropped onto it. She leant forwards and gazed deep into Annabelle's eyes as she sat across the table from her. "Love and the good Lord may take care of you after the wedding. But until then, it's just you, me, and the comfort of a thorough, diligently mapped-out plan." Philippa tapped a finger on the papers between them.

Annabelle looked at her church bookkeeper, smiled meekly, and took a long sip of tea. Her wedding may be akin to a battle of monumental proportions, and she fancied herself a warrior queen, but Philippa was her general. With a resigned expression, Annabelle said, "Okay. What would you like me to do?"

CHAPTER THREE

"IF POSSIBLE, MAKE a U-turn." The voice of the very nice English lady coming from his GPS was getting increasingly agitated, at least that's how it sounded to Father John. "If possible, make a U-turn."

The priest hunched over the steering wheel of his hire car and stared at the five-bar gate ahead of him. "If possible, make a U-turn." He gritted his teeth.

"I would if I could, mate," he told the GPS. He looked around him. Hedges hemmed him in. Ahead, on the other side of the gate was a field, ploughed and impassable. He was stuck. The only way out was to reverse up the track the very nice lady had sent him down. In error, it would seem. Father John banged his fingertips on his steering wheel and sat back. His had been a very long, distressing journey, and it wasn't over yet.

He'd left London at six a.m. that morning, well rested and keen to avoid the rush hour as he prepared to make the journey to Upton St. Mary, a place he'd never visited before, a journey he'd never made before. Five hours later, after many a traffic jam due to roadworks, incorrectly parked vans, and far too frequently absolutely nothing at all, he was lost, trapped in a very particular kind of rural maze. His throat parched, the passenger seat was strewn with wrappers, used napkins, and empty cartons that had contained provisions to sustain him on his long journey but were now long gone. He rustled through them, hoping to find something that would soothe his frayed nerves. A stray chocolate bar would do, or a bottle of water, but all he found was a lone cherry tomato. That wouldn't do at all. He threw it out of the window, a bright red berry landing in a sea of green.

Father John didn't normally drive. He got around London on public transport. He was an expert on the underground and buses. He could tell anyone how to get anywhere—the line, the number, where to get on, get off, and change. Even when he left the capital, he did so by train. But when he'd checked the timetables and planned out his journey to Upton St. Mary, he soon found that it would stretch to more than one day, a prospect he wasn't willing to countenance. And so, for the chance to officiate at her wedding and make Annabelle happy, he'd decided to rent a car, arrive a few days early, and enjoy the country parish seat for which she had left London and subsequently made her home.

He folded his arms. A raven laughed at him from a branch in an oak tree. There was another reason he'd wanted to get to Upton St. Mary early. He'd become concerned after his last call with Annabelle. She seemed more anxious, less happy-go-lucky than normal. It wasn't like her. He wanted to find out what was on her mind, offer her some of his premarital thoughts, calm her nerves, and perhaps give her tips on balancing the needs of a parish with a new relationship. But mostly, he simply wanted to spend time with her. It had been a long while since they'd last seen each other, and he knew that being in her company was the only way to truly know her.

Like everyone who encountered Annabelle, Father John cared deeply about her. He recognised and appreciated her earnestness, her warmth, her kindness and concern for all those she knew. And, sooner or later, those feelings were always returned. People couldn't help themselves. Annabelle was beloved. Father John had known her since she was a novice priest in her first post, and he had happily watched her progress. He had approved of how she had settled in her own parish, developed her relationships, and furthered God's work in her own inimitable style. She was unconventional, he'd give her that, but her methods worked, and she had built a strong community around her that was second to none.

Sighing, John put the car into reverse and wrapped his arm around the passenger seat headrest as he pivoted to look over his shoulder. He'd passed a farmyard a few hundred feet back. He could turn in there. There wasn't a soul around, and he slowly bumped his way back up the rough track until he was level with the entrance to the yard and the farm buildings that surrounded it. He pulled in, the wheels slipping on the slick surface of the hundreds of cobbles that had provided traction for farm vehicles and animals over decades, but which currently needed a good rinsing.

He drove his small hatchback into a corner next to a cow barn and once again looked over his shoulder to reverse into the second of his three-point turn. He aimed for the wide opening of the huge, windowless building behind him, blinking into the dark abyss inside. He could see only shadows, various shades of black and grey, and glimmers of upright, angular cow pens occasionally sliced through with daylight from gaps in the corrugated iron roof.

He reversed slowly, backing into the cowshed to give him plenty of space for his next manoeuvre. The car stopped. Frowning, Father John pressed gently on the accelerator. He felt resistance. Had he hit something? He looked skywards. The first five hundred pounds of any repair bill was on him before the car insurance kicked in. Climbing out, he walked along the side of the car, picking his way carefully across the greasy manure and straw-strewn cobbles. He peered into the gloom. There was a sack of feed up against his back wheels. Muttering quietly, he bent down to move it.

Only the ravens heard his sharp intake of breath. Father John staggered to the barn opening and reached out to steady himself on an old, craggy, woodworm-riddled upright post, gasping for air. Outside the sun was bright, the sky clear, the air crisp. But inside, darkness saturated everything with gloom, the air so thick it clogged his nostrils. Father John took one more look back and reached for his phone. The misshapen lump on the floor wasn't a sack of feed. It was a woman. A dead one, a pitchfork thrust through her chest.

CHAPTER FOUR

PHILIPPA PULLED A notebook from her cardigan pocket and licked a pencil tip as she gazed at its contents.

"Let's see . . . Today we're expecting Father John from London. Your brother Roger, niece Bonnie, and her friend Felicity are coming from Scotland. And Mary is arriving from France."

"How wonderful!" Annabelle said, beaming. "We should have them all for tea!"

Philippa wagged her finger at her. "There's no time for that! You will be busy. We'll have Father John and Mary over for dinner. They can join you and the inspector. The girls will be too tired. Now listen, we must have Mrs. Shoreditch over—we need to check your dress still fits. And you have to visit Mrs. Applebury about the flowers—she still has no idea which you'd prefer. Villagers have been growing them for you specially in the hope that you will choose theirs for your bouquet."

Annabelle slapped her forehead with her palm. "The pressure!"

"There's a lot riding on this wedding, Annabelle. There's a lot of potential for hurt feelings. It's not just about you, you know."

"Philippa, it isn't about me at all!"

Philippa looked at her list again. "There's also the wedding cake. Katie Flynn is bound to create something wonderful, but you need to visit her and make sure everything's to your liking. You also need to drive to the spa to confirm the food and timings with Sophie and Gabriella . . ."

Philippa's voice receded into the background as Annabelle's attention wandered. In those exhilarating days after she had accepted Mike's extravagant proposal, she had thought of married life plenty, envisioning long evenings spent gazing at each other over home-cooked dinners, mutually appreciated wine, and the comfort of their shared home. She had considered how soothing it would be to grow old together, to share experiences, and to support each other in whatever lay ahead.

But whilst Annabelle thought of marriage in terms of a long, extended future, Philippa thought only of the beginning. The wedding. A single occasion that needed to be strategised, sculpted, and polished to perfection. Annabelle saw herself as a wife-to-be, but Philippa considered her a bride. And it was this difference which had caused more than a little friction between them in recent days. Annabelle simply couldn't focus on what she considered trivialities. The question of the number and type of hors d'oeuvres served at the reception or who should sit next to Mrs. Beadle and her flatulence problem didn't interest her at all. Her concerns with the marriage lay elsewhere.

Philippa caught the glazed look in Annabelle's eyes. She had her chin propped on the heel of her palm and looked as if she were about to fall asleep. "Are you listening?" Philippa snapped. She had been reciting from a long list of action items in a particularly sonorous droning tone. Annabelle snapped to attention so quickly, it was clear she had dozed off, even if her eyes were open.

"Yes," Annabelle said, blinking. Philippa groaned in defeat. Annabelle pushed her chair back and got up. "Philippa, you're worrying too much. The wedding will be fine, whatever the flavour of cake or whichever colour of flower Mrs. Applebury chooses. I'm still the vicar of Upton St. Mary, you know. I can't abandon my duties for the sake of my wedding."

"I see," Philippa said with a sniff. She followed Annabelle out of the kitchen and into the living room. "I hope that'll comfort you when your guests have no place to sit, the bridesmaids arrive halfway through the ceremony, the reception is held in the rain, the flowers wilt on the tables, and the cake is soggy and stale by the time you cut it!"

Annabelle laughed lightly. She gently gripped the smaller woman's shoulders and looked her squarely in the face. "The wedding will be fine. I don't want a fuss. You've done enough. Let's just leave it at that."

"But . . . But . . . your dress . . . The order of service . . . The font for the seating plan . . ." Philippa clenched her jaw, too frustrated to finish her sentences and too perplexed by Annabelle's casual manner to find the words for a more characteristic sharp retort. She paused, but before she had gathered enough sense to speak, Philippa was interrupted by several short, sharp presses of the doorbell.

"Would you get that, Philippa?" Annabelle said.

Glowering, Philippa marched to the door and opened it

to reveal the tall figure of the bridegroom that was haunting her nightmares—Inspector Mike Nicholls.

"Hello, Philippa," he said sombrely. His eyes flitted across her face as he assessed the atmosphere of the cottage. One could never be too sure what was going on behind Annabelle's front door. It paid to check.

"Mike!" Annabelle called from inside.

"Hello," he said, relaxing a little. He smiled as he moved past Philippa to embrace his fiancée.

"What are you doing here so early? I wasn't expecting you until this evening."

Mike sighed. "Actually, I came to tell you I won't be free for dinner tonight as we'd planned."

"Why-ever not?"

"A body has been found in a barn south of the village." Mike winced. "Pretty gruesome, by all accounts."

"Who?" Philippa asked, her eyes widening.

Mike arranged his features, knowing that when he announced the name of the victim, Annabelle and Philippa would almost certainly know them. "I'm sorry to say that Kathleen Webster has been found dead."

"Oh my!" Philippa gasped, covering her mouth. Annabelle raked his features for some sign he was mistaken.

"Did you know her?" he said.

"A little, to say hello to. She didn't attend church, but I would see her around the village. Philippa might have known her better."

Philippa pursed her lips. "The Webster sisters are very reclusive. I've only nodded at Kathleen. Sometimes, her sister Joan used to come to the knitting circle and the WI after she was widowed but stopped a few years back. Something about her knee she said."

"I'm heading over to Webster's Farm now. Harper Jones

is there already. Apparently, she has some connection to the victim. The case is already more complicated than I'd like."

"And so close to the wedding!" Philippa was appalled.

"Yes, I want things cleared up quickly, so I need to act fast. I'll be working around the clock if necessary."

"I'm coming with you," Annabelle blurted out suddenly. "Just hold on there. I'll get dressed and we can go together."

"Annabelle, no, really. I'm sure you have other things to do," Mike called out. But Annabelle had already disappeared, and he knew she'd made up her mind. He looked down at Philippa staring at him sourly.

"Great," Philippa said. "Another excuse. That's all she needs."

CHAPTER FIVE

THE INSPECTOR'S BLUE Ford zipped along the narrow country lanes at a rapid clip. Annabelle gazed lazily out of the passenger window as the dewy fields, the first blooms of April, and the budding trees turned into a blur of bright green and flashes of colour.

Annabelle loved spring. The increasingly warm weather meant she could spend more time in the countryside appreciating the sight and scents of crab apple, cherry, hawthorn, and pussy willow blossoms; the bush-hopping of nesting swifts, swallows, martins, and sparrows; and the sky-sweeping flocks of migrating geese that entranced her anew each year. After the cold, wet days of winter, it was now just about warm enough to eat an ice cream if the sun came out, whilst soul-enriching stews and hearty log fires kept the evening chill at bay.

Seasonal transitions had always felt very spiritual to Annabelle. Indeed, she often referred to them in her sermons. It was for this very reason that she had chosen April for her wedding to Mike. A new beginning for her, for them, and for the world around them. Yet the closer the wedding date drew, the more she noticed the renewal of the countryside as it bloomed and budded once more, and the more disquieted she felt. The gripping, tense exchanges with Philippa hadn't helped, either. Even now, in the passenger seat of Mike's car, Annabelle felt an awkwardness which she could only resolve by ascribing it to the fact that she preferred driving herself, along with the unsettling news of Kathleen Webster's death.

"Is everything alright?" Mike said.

Annabelle turned from the window to smile at her future husband. "Oh yes. I'm just a little shocked. By the death, I mean."

Mike nodded. "I didn't expect you to come along . . ." Mike stopped himself. He knew very well that Annabelle couldn't stay away from something as dramatic as a sudden death any more than a bee could stay away from nectar. "I supposed that you would be busy planning the wedding," he added. "Only a few days now!"

"There's plenty of time yet," Annabelle said. She sounded as unconvinced as she felt. "Whoa!" Mike took a corner so fast the car slipped slightly on the curve, pushing Annabelle against the passenger door and forcing her to grab the handle above it. "Brake, drop down a gear, accelerate out," she said. Mike flicked a wary glance over at her before focusing quickly on the winding road ahead. "You need to learn how to handle a car around these tight country lanes, Mike."

Mike's eyes narrowed and he changed the subject. "Do you know anything about the Webster sisters that could help me?"

"Well," Annabelle said. She lifted her chin, a little of her typical fortitude returning. "They live on a smallholding—rather quaint but hidden away. They keep to themselves. Very rarely do they actually come into the village. They even have their shopping delivered—a bit avant-garde for these parts."

"Any reason they're reclusive?" Mike asked.

"Not really." Annabelle shrugged, shaking the hair out of her eyes now that the car was back on a level plane. "It's fairly common for people outside the village to like their privacy. That's why they live there. There's no privacy if you live in the village. None. Everything is everyone's business, or they like to think it is. If people don't know what's going on, they make things up. Anyhow, I think the smallholding has been in the Webster family for generations."

"Aren't they a bit old for farm work?"

"They're tough old birds. They work it with the help of the odd farm labourer or seasonal worker who stops by. Slow down. Take this country path." She pointed. "It's a good shortcut."

Mike took in the rolling hills and thickets of trees as the car's wheels bobbed over the uneven ground, not at all sure he should have taken Annabelle's advice. "Seems a quiet spot," he muttered. "Do you think we'll get there ahead of the villagers?"

"I wouldn't count on it. They probably heard about it before you did. And how long has it taken you to drive from Truro?"

"An hour."

"There'll be a welcome party for you, then.

"Annabelle, there's one thing about this case." Mike flicked another glance over at her.

"Oh?"

"If I can get a quick resolution, it might mean a promotion. That chief inspector role I was telling you about. The promotion board is sitting after we come back from honeymoon."

"Oh."

"That'd be good, wouldn't it? More money, but less time out in the field."

The car emerged from between some trees. Ahead stood a cluster of farm buildings tucked into a valley between two hills. A crowd of at least twenty lingered at the gate.

"How on earth do they do it?" exclaimed Mike as he steered the car off the path and towards the buildings. "Telepathy? I doubt a cow could sneeze without everyone at the other end of the village knowing about it instantly." He gave a quick toot of his horn to alert a family of five walking obliviously in front of him. "Anyhow, the promotion, that's what I've been thinking."

"Sounds great." Annabelle turned to him and beamed. She leant over to give him a kiss on the cheek. "I'm sure you'll walk it."

"Got to solve this case first. Let's see what's what, shall we?"

CHAPTER SIX

MIKE PARKED THE car on a grass verge and got out. He scanned the murmuring crowd for the officer in charge. Ahead of them, a few people stood at the entrance to a large barn, jostling to catch a glimpse of what was inside. Others mingled quietly in small groups farther away, exchanging gossip and muttering as they speculated on what might have happened. Mike grew increasingly angry.

"Hey, you!" he called out to a baby-faced man in a police officer's uniform that looked two sizes too big for him.

"Um . . ." the policeman said, his eyes frantic. He was overwhelmed. "Sir, I'm afraid you'll have to leave here. This is a . . . um . . . You'll have to go." That his words clearly made no impression on anyone around him was not lost on the young officer, and he showed no sign that he expected his instruction to be followed.

Mike scowled until Annabelle's gentle hand on his arm took the edge off his frustration. He restrained himself from giving the young officer an earful. "This is Inspector Mike

Nicholls of Truro Police," Annabelle explained. Mike waved his police ID.

"Oh!" the young man said, stiffening and saluting awkwardly. "Ah! I've . . . We've been waiting for you."

"Who are you?" Mike asked, squinting.

"Police Constable Derbyshire, Inspector."

"New, presumably."

"Yes, sir. A couple of weeks out of Hendon."

"Your first death?"

"Um . . . Yes, sir."

Mike looked around at the loitering crowd. "And you were sent to handle a crime scene by yourself?"

"No. Constable Raven came with me, sir."

"And where is Constable Raven?"

Derbyshire looked in the direction of the outbuildings that stood adjacent to the farmhouse. He pointed with a quivering finger. "He's trying to preserve the crime scene from . . . a cow, sir."

Mike looked over, squinted some more, then noticed what the young man was pointing at. Constable Raven was busy trying to drag a hapless Friesian cow out of a barn, the crowd around him only adding to the animal's reluctance. Mike dropped his head and rubbed a rough hand over his face. Annabelle smirked as she rubbed his arm. "Country life, Mike."

"How on earth did all these people get to the crime scene so quickly?" Mike asked.

PC Derbyshire shrugged. "There were a bunch of kids playing football just on the hill there. I suppose they came down when they saw our police car. Then Farmer Tremethick and his three dogs came over. The next thing we knew, there were loads of people. They must've messaged the news on their mobile phones. Village gossip travels like wildfire."

Mike sighed. "No secrets in the age of technology, I suppose," he grumbled as Annabelle once again patted him on the arm. He looked around at the crowd. He eyed a big man wearing a vest that exposed his tattoo-laden arms. The man seemed to take up as much space as the two people next to him. Mike shook his head. "What a shambles," he muttered. His expression took on a hard, commanding look, something Annabelle found terribly attractive so long as it wasn't accompanied by a taciturn mood. "Right, Derbyshire. Get rid of these gawpers. We've got work to do."

"But sir," Derbyshire said, in a trembling voice. He seemed even more overwhelmed than when they had found him. "I can't find the police tape!"

"What do you need police tape for, man? You're an officer of the law! Get to it! A strong, authoritative order is all you need. Crowd control. Police Basic Training, Day Three, Module Two. And er, good job on stopping me from coming in."

Derbyshire nodded vigorously. "Right, sir." He raised his voice. "Come on, people. Move please." He began shooing the onlookers away as if they were escaped sheep and not random passers-by. Like sheep, the crowd ignored his flapping hands. "Please."

The crowd took no notice. They were only roused into action when Mike strode amongst them, shouting, "Move it! I want everyone away! Anyone still here in thirty seconds will be charged with obstruction!" His booming order echoed around the valley, causing the crowd to stop their gawping and twittering. They scattered like a swarm of startled pigeons. The inspector made his way to the barn. "Macabre vultures," he muttered quietly to himself.

"Annabelle!" Annabelle looked over, surprised to hear the calling of her name. She immediately recognised Father John's bushy beard and twinkling eyes, above which lay eyebrows as bushy as the hairiest caterpillar. Her heart leapt. "Father John!" she cried. She ran towards him and hugged him warmly. "What on earth are you doing here?"

"It's good to see you, Annabelle." John stood back to smile at his former protégée, so much more experienced and worldly than when she was placed under his tutelage years ago. She was a little older, there were a few more laughter lines around her eyes, a few more inches around her middle, but it was the same irrepressible Annabelle who grinned back at him.

His smile disappeared quickly. "I've had quite a day. I had no idea how"—he searched for the right word—"active things are in the countryside."

"How so?" Annabelle asked, noticing the dark circles under Father John's eyes and hearing the grumbling of his stomach. "Are you alright?"

"Oh yes, I'm fine. Just a little tired and hungry, that's all. It's these newfangled machines. I do my best, but really! My GPS sent me down this lane to a dead end. I managed to pull into the farmyard to turn myself around and I stumbled on her, God rest her soul."

"You found the body? Kathleen Webster?"

Father John sighed. "Indeed. I called the police, and well"—he swung his arm around the farmyard—"here we are. I didn't expect to see you here."

"Mike is the investigating officer, so I said I'd come and see what's what. When these things happen in my community, I like to know what's going on."

"Happen a lot, do they?"

Annabelle gave a small smile. "Now and again." She looked over to the barn where she could see the inspector talking with the pathologist. "Was it gruesome?" Annabelle asked.

"It was rather. Not what I expected when I left London early this morning. I suppose you'll want to see for yourself."

"Come on, let's do it together."

CHAPTER SEVEN

ANNABELLE TOOK FATHER John's arm and they walked to join the others who were standing around Kathleen Webster's body. When Annabelle's eyes adjusted to the gloom, she gasped and put a hand over her mouth. A shivering chill stiffened her spine. A couple of goats munching hay casually observed the human chaos swirling around them, unperturbed.

A brown sack covered most of the body, but her face was exposed. That the victim was Kathleen Webster was unmistakable. What was even more unmistakable was the pitchfork driven through the sacking, and the body, apparently pinning it to the floor. Dried brown bloodstains surrounded the tines of the pitchfork and soaked into the sacking like a particularly challenging Rorschach test.

"Oh my . . ." Annabelle whispered. Father John let go of her hand and wrapped an arm around her shoulders. Annabelle looked at Harper Jones. The pathologist, known for her no-nonsense approach, scowled at the body, then at Annabelle. She was stoic, but Annabelle remembered what Mike had said about Harper having a connection to the dead woman. The vicar was probably the only person who noticed the pathologist's glistening eyes and trembling fingers. "Would you like to take a moment?" she asked Harper gently. "Or hand over to someone else?"

"No," the woman said, shaking her head. "I'm okay." Annabelle gazed into her eyes for a moment and placed a hand on Harper's arm. She felt Harper convulse. Annabelle continued. "You have a connection to . . . the victim."

Harper nodded slowly. "Webster is my maiden name. She is . . . Kathleen was my aunt. Joan is too, obviously."

"Joan Penberthy?"

"Yes, Aunt Kathleen's sister. She's in the house now."

Mike was listening to their exchange. His instinct was to butt in and ask about Joan's viability as a suspect, but he caught Annabelle's eye and noticed a tiny shake of her head. "What can you tell me?" he asked gently.

Harper shrugged helplessly. "I'm waiting for the team still, and we'll have to run some tests, but I can tell you it happened last night sometime—between six p.m. and six a.m. would be my guess. Signs of a minor struggle," she said, pointing at the scuff marks in the hay on the floor. "But it's a mess in here, what with the animals. Anyhow, she was dead before the pitchfork . . . ." Harper inhaled. "It didn't penetrate far, not to do any real damage, not much blood even; more cosmetic really." There was a brief pause as she gulped. "But I can't tell for sure until I have a better look at her."

Mike nodded. "Are you sure?"

"Yes!" Harper said sharply. "I'll deal with it. I wouldn't want anyone else."

"But this is terrible!" Annabelle exclaimed, unable to contain her horror any longer. "She was your family,

Harper, and this is . . . This is . . ." She looked around wildly at Mike, anyone, for help.

"A witch's death," came a deep voice from the entrance to the barn.

The group turned to see a heavyset, dark-haired man wearing an outfit that suggested he would be more at home in a field shooting pheasant, his guns handed to him by his loader, than standing over a dead body in a scruffy, careworn barn. He was wearing a wax jacket over a shirt and tie and green corduroys. On his feet were green wellies. He leant against a stall.

"What are you doing?" Mike called out, stomping towards him accusingly. "You have no business being here. Be gone!"

The man immediately held his palms up and shuffled backwards. "No problem, squire. I didn't mean any harm. I'll leave."

"No!" Annabelle called to him. "Wait. What did you just say?"

Unperturbed by the inspector's glare, the man said in a deep, cultured voice, "A witch's death. This"—he nodded at the body on the ground—"is a witch's death."

CHAPTER EIGHT

"THE PITCHFORK. IT'S symbolic."

"Tell us," Annabelle said. This strange man most definitely wasn't a local. She would know him.

"Back in the day, witches' bodies were often pinned to the ground with iron stakes after they had been executed. The purpose was to pin down the soul to make sure it couldn't return from the grave. Seems something similar's gone on here."

"How do you know this?" the inspector asked.

The man walked towards them. He had a bad limp and dragged his left foot against the straw-covered floor of the barn. "I'm a historian at the University of Warwick," he said as he slowly approached. "My name's Samuel Bellingham." The man offered his hand, but Mike didn't take it, his eyes searching Bellingham's face.

"Warwick, eh? What are you doing in Cornwall then?"

"I'm walking through the southwest of England recording unmapped landmarks and examining various formerly unremarked-upon features for a research project," Bellingham said, his baritone voice booming around the vast space of the barn. "Cornwall's a fascinating area, historically speaking. So much depth. I had hoped to be on my way to Land's End right now," he said, gesturing at his leg, "but I injured myself climbing Potter's Hill, so I'm stuck here for a day or two."

Mike grunted. "Still made it through the police cordon though, didn't you?"

"To be fair, Inspector, your defence was full of holes. A cow could have got through it." The sound of hooves clopping on cobbles accompanied the sight of PC Raven desperately trying to hold onto a rope fashioned into a halter around a cow's neck as it pranced clumsily in the yard outside.

"Potter's Hill gets terribly slippery. It's the clay soil," Annabelle said, anxious to head off another argument. "That's why it's called Potter's Hill. You know, clay . . ." No one acknowledged her. "Pots . . .?" she ended feebly and cleared her throat.

Bellingham smiled at Annabelle. "I see you have knowledge of the local area."

Mike pointed a finger into the air. "Look, you've no right to be here. Be off." He half-turned before hesitating. "But don't leave the village without telling me. I might need you again. Where are you staying?"

"The bed and breakfast on Tinny Lane. With Mrs. Sutton." The man limped off.

"I've a room with Mrs. Sutton too," Harper said. "For the wedding. Although I suppose I'll have more than that to concern myself with now this has happened."

"Okay, people" Mike said. "Harper, I'm sure your team can handle removal of the body. I'll stay with her until they arrive. Why don't you go into the house and check on your aunt?" Harper nodded, took one last look at the draped body, and left. "Annabelle," Mike said, "why don't you go with her? She looks like she could use a friend."

Mike noticed Father John for the first time. He looked at the priest's clerical collar and squinted as he searched his memory, unsure how to address the man but instinctively knowing it was important to find out before he said anything that might get him into trouble. He glanced at Annabelle.

"This is Father John. He's come for the wedding. He's going to conduct our service. Remember, I told you?" Annabelle explained, her eyebrows raised.

The inspector's shoulders relaxed, his face softened, and his eyes widened. "Ah, yes, sir, of course. I've heard a lot about you. Pleased to meet you." The two men shook hands. "But why are you in this barn? Shouldn't Philippa be plying you with tea and cake? You didn't travel all the way down here to look at a murder victim. You can't think much of our hospitality. Can we help you with anything?"

"I was on my way to the village when I got lost and found myself here, Inspector. I was on my way to Annabelle's cottage. I wasn't expecting quite such a . . . dramatic welcome. It was I who found the body."

"Really? Well, what jolly bad luck. I can assure you we aren't normally as . . . barbaric as this scene might suggest. Has one of my team taken a statement?"

"Yes, a Constable Raven, before . . . well, he got distracted by a nosy cow."

"Happens to us all, Father, happens to us all. Cows, yes." Mike seemed to be suffering from an uncharacteristic attack of nerves. He was babbling.

"Now, I just need help righting myself, perhaps with

some good old-fashioned directions, then I'll get out of your hair."

"Perhaps one of the villagers outside could help you? Or the constable? Although from the look of him, I couldn't guarantee it. Doesn't look like he could find his own backside, let alone the village." Mike folded his arms and pursed his lips.

"I could show you, if you like." All three of them jumped. Samuel Bellingham stood a few feet away.

"You still here?" Mike said.

Annabelle intervened quickly. "Could you? That would be fantastic, Mr. Bellingham."

"Thank you, young man," Father John said. "Let's get out of these good people's way. They have much more important things to worry about than my incompetence when it comes to technology." Father John shuffled around Annabelle and Mike to make his way out of the barn. "See you later, Inspector, Annabelle. Hopefully under better circumstances."

"Dinner tonight at my cottage, Father. Eight o'clock. We can catch up then. I'll see you out to the road. Then I'll check on Harper. You okay in here on your own, Mike?" Annabelle inquired.

"Yes, yes, of course. You go. I'll catch up with you later."

Once they left, Mike put a palm to his forehead and closed his eyes briefly before snapping them open. He shoved his hands in his pockets as he bent at the waist to look closer at the body, thoughts swirling around his mind.

"A witch's death," he mumbled.

"Witches, sir?"

Mike looked up to find Constable Derbyshire standing next to him, the young man jumping back suddenly as the inspector looked him over.

"S-s-sorry," Derbyshire stuttered. "I thought you were talking to me. Have you got a suspect already?"

"Suspect? What are you talking about?"

"The witch, sir."

Mike looked from the young man to the body, then back again. "What witch?"

"The travellers, sir. In the fields yonder. There's a witch amongst them."

Mike grimaced. "Travellers? What are you blathering on about, Derbyshire?" He looked as though he might shake the young man by the shoulders but shook his head instead.

Stuck between the intense desire to end the conversation and the understanding that his superior wanted an explanation, Derbyshire stuttered and swallowed until he had enough courage to say what was on his mind. "You said 'witch,' sir, so I thought you were talking about the travellers. They've been camped outside the village for the past month, sir. There's a woman with them who they say can tell your fortune and make up love spells and do all sorts."

"Love spells?"

"Yes. I mean . . . I don't know. A friend of mine had her make one up for him . . ."

"Really?"

"Yes, sir."

"Did it work?"

"I hope so!" Derbyshire said, grinning before quickly stopping himself. "I mean . . . for his sake. He really likes this girl."

Mike nodded sceptically. "So, this woman . . . She's selling her services as a witch?"

"Yes . . . sort of . . . well, she calls herself a witch."

"Is that right?"

"Yes, sir."

"Where did you say they were camped?"

Mike looked to the fields beyond the barn's entrance where the young man pointed, his mind already working. "I suppose that's as good a place to start as any then."

CHAPTER NINE

HARPER STOPPED AT the door of the farmhouse, her hand on the doorknob. "I should warn you, Reverend, Aunt Joan is rather . . . confused a lot of the time."

"How so?" asked Annabelle.

"She's not been the same since her husband died. She can seem perfectly fine one moment, then say the most strange, outlandish things the next. Both of my aunts were a bit like that—unpredictable—but Joan far more so."

"I see," Annabelle said. "Well, I'm no stranger to odd behaviour, so don't worry." Harper nodded and opened the door.

The downstairs of the cottage was one large, open space. Annabelle thought it larger than it appeared from the outside. However, it wasn't a huge, rambling farmhouse; it was much smaller. Not as small as a labourer's cottage, though. The ancient stone brickwork was exposed, the walls bare of decoration. Two worn chairs arranged around an equally worn rug stood in front of the old fireplace. Pots, pans, and a few chains of onions hung from the ceiling. On the other side of the large room was the kitchen, divided from the rest by a long table. A coal-burning stove stood next to a stone counter, the likes of which Annabelle had not seen since she last visited a museum. There was a door in the corner behind which she suspected some rickety stairs led to the bedroom.

Aunt Joan sat at the kitchen table tearing crusty bread over a tin bowl filled with some kind of yellow soup. She wore an old Fair Isle-patterned sweater, the elbows reinforced with leather patches. A long paisley skirt skimmed the floor. Her feet were bare, the skin dark, cracked, and dirty, and her wiry, grey-black hair was roughly tied back with a red ribbon. Joan Penberthy looked as old and rustic as the farmstead, except for one thing. When she turned to her visitors, Annabelle saw that her eyes were clear and sharp, a soft yet penetrating hazel, green and golden like the emerging springtime. Just like Harper's.

"Harper, luvvie!" Joan called when she noticed the visitors. "Come and sit." She patted the chair next to her. "There's a little left if you want some!" She waved at a large pan of soup simmering on the stove. Harper and Annabelle exchanged a quick look. They approached the table, taking a seat each.

"No thank you, Auntie Joan. I'm fine."

"Are you sure?" Joan said with a smile, her teeth yellow and grey. She dipped a piece of bread into the thick yellow mixture three times. "It's very good." She leant over and loudly slurped soup from her spoon.

"Auntie," Harper said softly, reaching out a hand and placing it on the old woman's wrist. "Do you know what's happening?"

"Course I do, my dear. I'm eating my soup."

"No, Auntie Joan. Do you understand that Kathleen's gone?"

"Kathleen? Gone? Ha!" Joan said. "She's probably lost in the fields again, the silly mare! I keep telling her to take a map, but she listens to the cat more than me!"

"Auntie Joan, listen to me. She's dead. She died last night. You haven't seen her today, have you now?"

Joan looked at her niece, the sparse light in the room highlighting the honey hues of the older woman's irises as she searched Harper's face. "Dead? Dead, you say?" she answered slowly, as if turning the words over in her mind to examine them for accuracy. She paused. The wrinkles in her forehead suddenly relaxed and her eyebrows dropped. She focused her attention back to her soup. "Well, there you go. No one's immune." She slurped her soup again. Harper's lips pressed into a thin line.

"Joan, do you remember anything about last night?" Annabelle asked.

"Last night? Oh, I wasn't here," the old woman said. She lifted her soup-laden spoon to her mouth and blew on it.

"What do you mean? Where were you?" Harper asked.

"I took the bus to Truro."

"Truro?"

"Yes," Joan said, staring into the distance. "It was the queerest thing. I waited an hour for the bus, sat on it for an hour and a half." She waved her soup spoon in the air. "We went through St. Mawseth, Cadbrear, Gwingarne, Folly's Bottom . . ."

"Yes, Auntie, we know."

"Such a long way round and hardly anyone gets on. And it was only when I got off in the city that I remembered—"

Harper covered her face with her hand. "That Penny

moved to Manchester a year ago. Penny is my cousin, Joan's daughter," she explained to Annabelle.

"Yes!" the old woman said. "How about that! It was too late to get the return bus, so I wandered around and came back this morning."

"You walked around Truro all night? By yourself?"

Joan shrugged. "What else was I going to do? I'll tell you something though. That journey certainly built up my appetite! Are you sure you don't want any of this soup? It's dandelion and dill. Delicious."

CHAPTER TEN

"**D**ID KATHLEEN KNOW you were gone?" Harper asked.

"Probably not. She was out in the barn when I left. We'd had one of our barneys." Joan sniggered. "Get that? Barney? Barn? Anyway, I was fed up with Kath, so I thought, I fancy going to see Penny. I got my bus pass and off I went. Just like that. Truth be told, it was all a bit of fun. An adventure. Kath was doing the evening feed, so I left her to it." Joan smiled and her eyes twinkled as she revisited the memory of what Annabelle suspected was something of a rare rebellion.

"I thought you had a farmhand do the feeds. You're too old to be doing that kind of thing," Harper chided.

"Farmhand?" Joan said, momentarily confused before her bright eyes lit up with understanding. "Oh! We got rid of that horrible fellow last week. Terrible chap! What was his name again?" Joan screwed up her face and stared into her dandelion and dill soup, stirring it slowly. "Ah, yes!" she cried, raising her soup spoon like it was a flag. Drops of thick yellow liquid sprayed across the table. "Neil, that's it. Awful, he was."

"Awful? How?" Joan fixed Annabelle with an unflinching gaze. It occurred to the vicar that the flecks of colour in Joan's eyes matched that of her soup.

"Why? Because he was useless, of course! The animals hated him. They'd kick out and knock over the feed. Made a right mess of the place. And the cat! I've never heard her hiss so much!" She looked around. "Where is that cat? Haven't seen it all morning." Harper touched her fingers lightly. "What? Oh yes, and he was awful to be around, kept moaning all the time. I can't be doing with moaners."

"What was he moaning about?"

"Oh, you know, this and that. The cows, me and Kath, the cat. Kath thought he had some problem with females—any kind—man or creature. And oh! Some bother about a wedding or other. He went on and on about that."

Harper looked over at Annabelle. The vicar remained impassive, but a slight crease appeared between her eyes and the lines around them deepened as she listened. "Did he mention whose wedding?" Harper asked.

"Oh, I don't know. I don't pay attention to people who talk nonsense," Joan said, breaking off another piece of bread and wiping it around her plate.

Harper sighed and stood up from the table. "Alright, Auntie Joan. I'm just going to go upstairs and look through a few of Kathleen's things."

"Take whatever you want," Joan said. "Take the cat as well. You'd be doing me a favour."

"Annabelle, would you like to give me a hand?" Harper's eyes widened as she nodded to the door in the corner of the room. Annabelle stood from the table.

"We'll be back in a few. One last thing, Mrs.

Penberthy," Annabelle said. "What did you and your sister have an argument about?"

"Argument?"

"Yes, your barney with Kathleen. What was it over?"

"Can't remember."

"Try, Auntie Joan. It might be important," Harper added.

"Probably nothing. We were always arguing. Me and Kath, just a couple of crabby old women getting on each other's nerves." For the first time, Joan showed some emotion over her sister's death. Her eyes moistened. "I'll miss her though," she added softly.

Harper opened her mouth to urge her on, but Joan headed her off. "Alright, alright, shush a minute. Let me think; it'll come back to me." Joan gazed into the distance, scraping the bowl fruitlessly with her spoon as Annabelle and Harper waited. "Nope, it's completely gone. Sorry," she said, clearly not sorry at all. She tipped her head back and lifted the bowl to her mouth, draining it of the remnants of her soup. Annabelle smiled. That's what she'd do too, in the circumstances.

🌍

Harper led Annabelle up the rickety staircase to the bedroom. Two single beds sat in perfect symmetry on either side of the room, a single nightstand between them, shelves above their headboards laden with books, a plastic flower in a small vase, and an old alarm clock circa 1970. Two grimy windows, opposite each other on either side of the room, let in some light—just. Faded floral curtains hung at their sides. In one corner, sitting on a dresser was a china bowl and a tall yellow jug decorated with daisies. In the other there stood a bulky oak wardrobe, the handle of a small key sticking out of the lock. The only evidence of modernity—a shiny, new electric heater—was placed in the middle of the room.

Annabelle looked around. "Where's the bathroom?" she asked Harper.

"What? Oh, that's outside. As you can probably tell, my aunts aren't for newfangled things. They were quite happy with a privy in the garden."

"Bit cold in the winter." Annabelle stepped further into the room. "What do they do at night?"

"Chamber pots under the bed. Just like the good old days." In a low voice, Harper said, "I'm terribly sorry, Annabelle. This all must seem rather grim."

"All in a day's work," Annabelle remarked, waving away Harper's apology. "There's still a few around here with an outside toilet." To spare Harper's feelings, Annabelle failed to mention that they had all been converted to sheds.

Harper sighed and sat on one of the beds, her shoulders slumping. "I tried to get them to move a while back. This farm was just too much for them, and they became more and more isolated, untethered from reality. The travelling and wandering around in the night is new though. It's worrying. Joan forgets things. But then at other times, she's as sharp as a tack."

Annabelle moved over to the pathologist whom she admired for being so together, in control. She thought back to the time she first met Harper, at the death of a newcomer who had moved into Woodlands Manor. Annabelle had been new to the area, and she had felt out of her comfort zone, overwhelmed. Then, Harper seemed so confident and inspiring that Annabelle would have happily changed places with her. Now though, she was vulnerable.

Annabelle put her arm around the older woman's shoulders tenderly. Harper gave Annabelle a weak smile.

"Are you going to be okay, Harper? I know you've never been the most religious person, but that's no reason to reject the chance to talk openly occasionally. I'm here if you need me."

"Thank you, Annabelle. I appreciate it. I'm fine though, really. I've seen enough dead bodies and enough grieving family members to feel well prepared for this."

Annabelle nodded sympathetically. "There's no shame in feeling sad, though. It's different when it's someone you love. Just remember that."

Harper allowed her cool, competent exterior to melt for a few seconds, slumping against Annabelle before, with a sniff, she roused herself and stood. "Gosh, I'm so sorry, Reverend. This is a terrible way to spend the run-up to your wedding! You should be doing happy things, thinking happy thoughts!"

"Ah well, I may be getting married, but I've still got a parish to look after!"

"And you've still got an appetite for solving mysteries, it seems," Harper said, looking about the room.

"I prefer to think of it as taking an active role in my future husband's career and the well-being of my parish." Annabelle smiled. "Now, how can I help?"

CHAPTER ELEVEN

"THIS IS MY Aunt Kathleen's side of the room." Harper held up her left arm and indicated to the right wall with the other. The bed's candlewick bedspread lay over candy-striped sheets and was topped with a motley collection of faded, threadbare cushions. "I'd like to give the whole house a good cleanup, but perhaps we should start with her things first. There might be something here that could help shine some light on what happened."

"Good idea," Annabelle responded.

For the next twenty minutes, the two women scoured the room. At first, it seemed as if there was little to pick through; the items the women possessed were either old, cheap, or both. But as they delved deeper into cupboards, crannies, and cardboard boxes, they soon found that Aunt Kathleen's belongings contained numerous secrets and surprises. Tatty photos fell from books as they were plucked from shelves, and opened shoeboxes revealed delicate, sparkling costume jewellery. Pockets held all manner of handwritten notes, lists, bits, and bobs.

Nothing struck them as particularly noteworthy,

however, until Annabelle lifted Kathleen's mattress and pulled an old notebook from the springs. "Harper," she gasped. "Look at this."

The pathologist moved to peer over Annabelle's shoulder, one of the few women in Annabelle's life tall enough to do that. They both looked down at the battered book. The cover was an acid yellow. One corner had been ripped away, revealing elaborate cursive on the pages inside. The edges of the cover were faded and beaten; the spine was covered in brown fabric.

"It looks very old," Annabelle said.

"I'm more accustomed to dating corpses than books, but this looks almost certainly over a hundred years old—perhaps even older. Look, there's a date here." Harper pointed to a mark in the corner. "Eighteen fifty-seven."

"Could it be a diary?" asked Annabelle.

"Possibly. Open it."

Carefully, Annabelle turned to the first page, the spine cracking as she did so. "The pages are very brittle. I'm frightened I'm going to damage them."

"Diary of Martha B. George," Harper read slowly from the first page. "Eighteen fifty-seven."

"Who's Martha B. George?"

Harper shrugged. "I've no idea."

Annabelle flipped to the next page. Large, loopy handwriting that sloped to the right at an acute angle filled the page from edge to edge. "Oh my!" Annabelle exclaimed. "How could anyone ever read that? It looks so fine and impressive, but it's hard to read."

"But neat. No crossings out, uniform lettering. She had great penmanship." Harper scrambled for a shopping list she had found in one of Kathleen's pockets, putting it alongside the book's pages for comparison.

"It looks genuine, and it's nothing like my aunt's handwriting. I wonder why she had it. And where it came from."

"And why put it there under her mattress? Did she ever mention it to you?"

"No, but it must have been important to her."

"Perhaps she was keeping it for someone? Or hiding it?"

"Difficult to know. My aunt wasn't the most logical of people, eccentric at best. She could have put it there for any reason. Might be nothing at all. Maybe she picked it up somewhere and stashed it there simply because it was convenient. She'd clearly run out of room on the shelves." Harper took the book from Annabelle's hands and closed it, brushing a finger gently against the torn cover. She turned it over. "We should show it to the inspector."

"I doubt he'll have the patience for it unless we have some reason to connect it with Kathleen's death." Annabelle put a finger to her lips as she considered the book. Her eyes widened.

"Come to supper at my cottage tonight," she said. "Bring the book with you. Father John will be there. He's very knowledgeable about history. He might be able to tell us something about it."

"Are you sure?" Harper said.

"Sure about you coming to dinner? Yes. Sure that Father John might be able to add something? No, but he has a particular love for old English poems, and his handwriting is terrible. If he can read his own writing, he'll almost certainly be able to decipher whatever's in here! Maybe he can help us make sense of this, even if it is a red herring."

"Do you know anything about this, Auntie Joan?" Harper asked her aunt when they went downstairs.

Joan was still sitting at the kitchen table. She'd finished her soup and her head nodded as she fought sleep. A night walking around Truro was tiring business. "What's that, dearie?"

"This." Harper showed her the notebook. Joan took it from her, and like Harper had done earlier, she turned it over in her hands, reading the words across the front and examining the back. "Well, well, well. I haven't seen this in years."

"You've seen it before?"

"Oh yes, when we were girls. I saw Kathleen read this before she went to sleep sometimes. Used to tuck it under her mattress like it was some kind of secret. She never told me what it was though, and I never asked."

"How long ago was this?"

"Ooh, a long time, years. We must have been about what, fourteen or so. About the time I came to your family. I haven't seen it recently though, at least not that I can remember. I didn't know she still had it. I think she said she found it under a floorboard once."

"And she never told you about it or why she had it?"

"No, never." Joan's eyelids flickered.

"Okay, Auntie Joan, that's all for now. Take care. I'll be back soon. I'm going to stay in the village for a bit."

"That'll be nice, luvvie. Perhaps Penny can come and keep you company. Truro's not far."

"She's not . . . never mind. Yes, maybe. I'll give her a call."

CHAPTER TWELVE

ALONG WITH THE mood, the bright spring day had turned overcast, the clouds blanketing the sun so that the air was chilly. Annabelle clutched herself tightly as she waited outside for Mike to conduct his own interview with Joan. As she waited, she watched the SOCO team working around and inside the barn. She felt a desperate need for a hot cup of tea, preferably accompanied by a slice of cake, maybe two, possibly three. She needed them to warm her up, cool her nerves, and settle her restless thoughts.

Eventually, Mike emerged from the house, pinching his lips together as he snapped his notebook shut and pocketed it. "How did it go?" Annabelle asked. "Did she say anything relevant?"

Mike growled. "Relevant? No. Though I know everything about her 'lucky cooking pot' and her belief that using a blue handkerchief will make colds worse."

Annabelle patted his arm sympathetically. "Let's go," she said.

Noticing the chill in the air and the way Annabelle's

arms were curled around herself, Mike said, "Would you like my coat?" His hands pulled at his lapels as he prepared to take it off and drape it around Annabelle's shoulders.

"Don't be silly," Annabelle said. "The car's right here."

Mike put his arm around her shoulder, rubbing it as he tried to instil some warmth into her, but Annabelle could sense the heavy thoughts going on behind that rough stubble and serious expression. When they reached the car, Annabelle turned back one last time to look across the farmyard as Kathleen Webster's body was placed into the back of a medical van. She pressed her fist to her lips sadly and looked over at Mike as he circled the car to open the driver-side door.

"You sure you won't be free to have supper tonight?" she asked.

Mike pursed his lips apologetically. "It doesn't look that way. Not unless you're eating at midnight. The first hours after a murder are key, and I want this wrapped up quickly."

"Never mind. I'll keep something back for you."

"Marvellous," Mike said, brightening as he got into the car. "I'll make myself at home at the station." He put the key in the ignition. "What do you think then? About this death?"

Annabelle raised her eyebrows as high as they would go. "Are you actually asking me for my opinion, Inspector?"

Mike laughed gently. "Your opinions are important. I wouldn't be marrying you if they weren't. And more pertinently, you wouldn't be marrying someone who didn't value your opinion, now would you? You're not daft. And neither am I. I know which side my bread's buttered on."

"Well, if you're asking my opinion as your future wife, I

think you should take plenty of breaks and not work yourself mad as you usually do."

"And your opinion as a wonderful, intelligent woman with a knack for spotting things that have helped me solve cases before?"

"Hmm." Annabelle had a think. "If we're assuming it is murder—"

"It is. There's no way someone could do that to themselves. There must have been a person on the other end of that pitchfork."

Annabelle winced at the brutality of the image his words conjured up, then returned to her thoughts. "Then I think an act so ghastly must have a terribly powerful motive behind it."

Mike nodded as he allowed an idea to brew in his mind. "Is there anything else you can tell me about Kathleen Webster? No one seems to know much, and her sister wasn't a lot of help."

"Not really, I'm afraid." Annabelle sighed. "Like I said earlier, they live isolated lives down here and are pretty self-sufficient with their animals and their vegetables. They use casual labour to help them out, people passing through rather than locals, so any knowledge of them tends to be lost quickly. The vet, Dr. Whitefield, might know something. They probably had to call him out from time to time."

"It's a strange case," Mike said, scratching his stubble. "Nothing stolen. A victim who seemed to have had little contact with the outside world. And yet such a violent, grisly murder. It almost feels personal, intimate."

"Something buried in the past, perhaps?"

"Perhaps," Mike said, his frown lines deepening. "What did you make of her sister Joan?"

Annabelle shrugged. "It's difficult to make any sense of

what she says. She doesn't seem terribly aware of what's going on around her."

"Huh, do you think she could've . . ."

Annabelle's raised her eyebrows. "You can't honestly be considering Joan a suspect!" she gasped.

"Why not? She's pretty much the only person who was close enough to Kathleen to have any sort of reason to kill her, and she didn't seem too concerned about her death."

"She was her sister!"

"So? In my experience, blood ties never stop people from doing horrible things to one another. Quite the opposite a lot of the time."

"She said she went to Truro last night."

"She also said that she owned a clock which told her the weather," Mike replied. "In words."

"She did say there was some animosity between the two of them."

"Well, there you are then."

"But that's probably just them being"—Annabelle thought back to what Joan had said—"crabby old women. Did she seem the murdering type to you? You who have so much experience in these types of things."

"Not that I could make out, but then I couldn't make out much about her at all. And you never know, resentments and grudges can go back decades. All it takes is one little thing, and snap!" Mike mimed a twig breaking in two. "Bob's your uncle. Or Joan's your aunt in Harper's case."

Annabelle rested her head against the seat, still frowning at the idea of Joan as a suspect. Mike started the car and guided it onto the road that would lead them back to the village. He would go via the regular route this time, like normal people did. As he drove the car into the lane from the barnyard, he saw the big man he'd seen earlier. He was standing on the grass verge, his arms folded over his swollen belly. He stared at Mike hard.

"She mentioned a cat," Annabelle murmured. The passing scenery stirred her thoughts. "But I didn't see it anywhere."

"Isn't that what cats do? Disappear until feeding time? I don't think that's relevant."

Annabelle smiled at his dismissal; Mike was very much a dog person. "I think their cat's missing. The bowl was full of untouched food that had dried over."

Mike waved away her concern with his hand. "It's probably doing what it does best. Off hunting mice somewhere."

Annabelle banged her head on the roof of the car. The soft spongy ceiling protected her, but she was dramatically jolted in her seat. "Hey!"

"Sorry," Mike said. He'd driven the car over a pothole with very little care.

"You're going to have to learn to drive these lanes a bit better than that when we're married."

"Sorry," Mike said again.

"I've just remembered something. A farmhand . . . Joan said they recently sacked a farm labourer."

Mike glanced at her, his eyes alight with interest. "And you told me about the cat before you decided to tell me that? She mentioned nothing about any farmhand to me."

CHAPTER THIRTEEN

"THEY GOT RID of him last week. That's why Kathleen was in the barn when she was murdered. She was tending the animals because they didn't have anyone else to do it. Joan didn't seem very fond of him, and said . . ." Annabelle paused, concerned by the memory. "She said he had been complaining a lot, particularly about 'some wedding or other.'"

Mike didn't speak for a few moments. "Could that have been her babbling? Conflating two things without any sort of connection?"

"I don't know."

"What was his name?"

"Neil. She couldn't recall his surname."

"Good enough," Mike said purposefully. "We'll find him if he's still around."

They made their way back to the church without incident, Annabelle silently pressing the phantom brake, clutch, and accelerator that existed in her footwell whenever she was a passenger. The clouds darkened over the course of their drive, threatening rain. St. Mary's church tower was shrouded in gloom.

When they arrived at Annabelle's gate, she undid her seatbelt. "Where are you off to now?"

"I'm going to stop off quickly at the station, give some marching orders about looking for this Neil person, then I'm going to speak to a group of travellers Derbyshire told me about. They should be good for a start."

"Travellers?" Annabelle exclaimed. "Why on earth are you going to see them?"

"That historian fellow at the crime scene—"

"Samuel Bellingham."

"Bellingham, yes. What he said about this looking like the killing of a witch got me thinking. Derbyshire said there's a witch at the travellers' encampment. It's a load of old nonsense, if you ask me, but I can't deny the connection. So, to the source of the nonsense I go." He glanced over at Annabelle. "What is it?"

She looked at him, a dubious pout on her lips. "They're a rather . . . defensive people, Mike, the travellers. I-I'm sure they're perfectly nice people individually, but there is tension between them and the villagers."

"What do you mean?"

Annabelle exhaled. The group of families that had arrived two months ago on the outskirts of Upton St. Mary was a difficult subject to broach, especially when you were the local woman of God. "They've caused rather a stir since they first settled here. The villagers have a deep dislike of them, and the feeling seems mutual. Farmers complained that they were settling on their property, parents complained that the young travellers were corrupting their children, and there was an incident that almost resulted in a riot when they rode their horses through the village centre.

Two of them were even held at the station for a couple of hours for a breach of the peace."

"That all sounds rather par for the course. There's always suspicion and resentment between locals and travellers."

"Perhaps." Annabelle sighed. "But they've been ordered to relocate several times now, and though there's not been much incident for a few weeks, feelings run high whenever they come up in conversation."

"Okay, but why should any of that concern me?"

"Well," Annabelle answered, "they don't seem to have much respect for the police. Understandable, I suppose, considering it's them who keep moving the travellers on. I've heard that they regard the police as their enemy in many respects. I'm sure they are all fine. It's just . . . I don't want anything to happen to you."

Mike reached out to grasp Annabelle's hand. "You don't sound like the Annabelle I fell in love with. Since when did your belief in the inherent goodness of people falter?"

"Since the possible lack of it threatened to harm my soon-to-be husband."

Mike smiled. "I'll be alright. But I appreciate the concern." He brought her hand to his mouth and kissed it.

"You're right," Annabelle said bashfully. "I've slipped. I shouldn't think the worst. In fact, I've been thinking of paying them a visit myself. You know, to bridge relations. I've just been preoccupied with other things lately."

She rubbed the back of her hand against the stubble on Mike's cheek and sighed as she looked over at the front door of her cottage. She felt her energy drain as she thought of what, and who, awaited her behind it, but without good reason to hang about, Annabelle opened the car door and got out.

"What are you having for supper?" Mike called out to her.

Annabelle poked her head back into the car. "Beef Wellington. I'll keep some for you."

"Are you doing it with—"

"The peas you like? Of course."

"Could you maybe put—"

"Gravy on the potatoes? Yes, dear."

"And—"

"Save the middle slice for you? Absolutely." Mike liked his beef rare.

Mike chuckled as she shut the door, and with a full heart and in anticipation of an even fuller stomach, he drove off, considering what a lucky man he was. Travellers, murders, and witches notwithstanding.

CHAPTER FOURTEEN

INSPECTOR MIKE NICHOLLS had very little time for superstitions, although in his increasing dealings with the villagers of Upton St. Mary, he had grown accustomed to hearing them. From farmer Leo Tremethick's belief that an overgrown marrow always preceded a decrease in milk prices to Mrs. Shoreditch's refusal to sew anything in black and yellow for fear she would get stung by marauding bees, this small corner of the Cornish countryside was fertile ground for active imaginations. The quiet, relaxed pace of life allowed plenty of time for the mind to wander.

Mike, on the other hand, was a man of logic, rationality, and principle. He felt it was the only way to live life. But where he had once dismissed beliefs that were not well and truly grounded in fact as the stuff of juvenile games and fairy tales, he now understood that something didn't have to be true for it to be considered true. And by many, at that.

And if it was considered true, you could bet it influenced behaviour. If Debbie Partridge believed that hearing a tortoiseshell cat meow on a Saturday night meant she was about to get sick, you would know that come Monday, she would be feeling poorly. If she wasn't, she would simply consider it a rare exception to the rule, or that she'd been protected by a cow with a particular pattern of markings that had crossed her path the day before, or something equally bizarre. She'd justify her belief somehow.

It was because of this new respect for beliefs in which he didn't believe that the comments made by Samuel Bellingham, the well-fed, lame hiker-historian he had met at the crime scene had stuck with the inspector. Superstition was fine enough when limited to harmless whims, but one taken to an extreme could easily result in an act as senseless. Could an unfounded belief be at the root of Kathleen Webster's murder?

The sky remained cloudy and dark when Mike parked his car next to a gate at the entrance to a field, some way from where he knew the travellers to be camped. The vast, open ploughed field beyond the gate was too bumpy and soft to take the car further. He would have to walk. Mike turned off the engine and got out, immediately tightening his coat about him as the damp, cold air whipped around his face, causing his lapels to flap. It may have officially been spring, but winter hadn't quite given up the fight yet. Hunched, he trudged towards the camp that he could just about see in the far distance, wincing as the wind slapped his cheeks. It seemed determined to battle him all the way across the field.

Mike counted eight modern, egg-shaped caravans parked at random angles to each other on a strip of grass at the far edge of the field, a traditional, tall, brightly painted horse-drawn wagon parked amongst them. They loosely formed a semicircle, trucks and four-wheel drives lined up neatly alongside. Plastic outdoor tables and chairs were strewn haphazardly, a couple on their sides, perhaps blown over by blasts of wind. A couple of grills stood at the edge of the camp.

He noticed a young girl caressing a sturdy chestnut horse some way from the camp. Another horse with black and white markings and heavily feathered white legs quietly grazed inside the semicircle between washing lines strung between the caravans. Tethered to a tree behind them, a huge black horse stood snorting and stamping a hoof.

As Mike drew closer, he saw several children in cheap, tatty clothing kicking a ball around in the wind. They were using rags, or possibly clothes, for goalposts. When the kids kicked the ball, Mike could hear from the dull thud that it was flat.

A sudden gust swung the children's deflated ball high towards him, eventually resting a few feet away. With the irresistible, instinctive delight of virtually every male in existence, Mike immediately forgot himself and abandoned his hunched gait. He opened up his body and took one perfectly timed stride towards the ball, side-footing it with a satisfying thwack. The ball left his foot elegantly, his kick firm enough to compensate for the lack of air inside it as it sliced through the wind. It curved just a little to land right in front of the children, bobbling as it rolled awkwardly a few feet.

Mike, pleased as punch with his technique and perfect placement, looked at the children, hoping for some applause, maybe a cheer. But the children were staring silently, stock-still, seeming, despite his unquestionable ball skills, to ignore his kick entirely. They were frozen, staring at him with expressions that were a mixture of curiosity, suspicion, and, in a few instances, terror. There was a second when both Mike and the kids paused, action and thought frozen across the divide. Mike thawed first and opened his mouth to speak, but before he could do so, the children spun around and took flight like a pack of wild animals, screaming as they scrambled towards their caravans, into which they disappeared. The melee caught the attention of adults who had been milling around chatting or getting on with chores, but who now stood, alert and appraising, their eyes fixed firmly on the stranger.

With a deep sigh, Mike hunched over again against the cold and ploughed onwards through the makeshift football pitch towards the camp. More people were climbing out of their caravans and now, as Mike counted twenty-five adult travellers watching him, the children's cries were replaced by an uneasy, brooding silence. He felt apprehensive as he remembered Annabelle's cautionary words and counted the dogs roaming the camp, assessing them for the threat they posed. Unconcerned chickens weaved amongst them.

"We're not moving again, copper," a booming voice called.

The giant man Mike had seen at the farm earlier stepped into his path, fifteen feet away. More akin to an upright bear than anything human, a long, bushy beard hung from the huge man's stern, brooding warrior-esque face. It was a beard that Mike suspected hadn't been the recipient of a sharp edge in several years. Once again, thick, tattooed arms lay across the man's powerful, protruding belly. Earrings dangled from his large ears. His head, in contrast with his face, was shiny and completely bald. The man formed a human barrier between the detective and the camp—a very effective one.

Mike wasn't surprised that the travellers recognised him as a police officer, despite his lack of uniform. He knew well enough that those who had regular run-ins with the law learnt to detect the signs: a particular gait, a certain dry detached expression, the authority that came with the power to detain and arrest. He drew to a halt. "I'm not here to move you on," he called out across the expanse between them.

"Then leave," the bear-man called out again, briefly flashing large, crooked teeth. "There's nothing for you here."

Mike paused and looked past the man's giant frame at the other travellers who were now gathered in small groups around the camp. They watched the interaction warily. Mike considered his next words carefully, knowing that mention of a murder would only inflame the tension between them. "I'm here to speak to a woman. One who deals in"—he stood up a bit taller—"witchcraft."

His words provoked murmuring amongst the camp members. Mike attempted to interpret how his comment had landed. He was unsure.

"Let him through, Dylan," a bright, sharp voice called from one of the caravans. Everyone looked towards the female voice. Mike saw an old woman, far older than her voice implied, standing in the doorway of the colourful wagon. Everything about the camp was practical and care-worn, from the clothes the travellers wore to their caravans. This wooden wagon was the exception. The roof was immaculately weatherproofed. A small chimney pipe stuck out from the top. The wheels, one large and one small on each side, were strong and perfectly round. The windows were spotless.

But what was most eye-catching was the decoration. The wooden caravan was freshly painted in panels of red and gold. Elaborate wood carvings of flowers ran along the sides. Below the entrance was a set of steps, a gracefully curved handrail carved in wood alongside it. Flowerpots filled with brightly coloured primroses stood on either side of the steps. On this grey day, amongst the shabbiness of the camp, the caravan stood out like a pair of brightly painted lips on a plain face. The elderly woman stood at her doorway, two feet higher than the inspector. She looked down at him and flashed a patchy smile—every alternate tooth seemed to be missing—her eyes focused on Mike. "He's harmless," she said.

CHAPTER FIFTEEN

THE BEAR-MAN and Mike returned each other's gaze, the air heavy with controlled male aggression. Finally, Dylan seemed to come to a decision. He stepped aside, watching Mike carefully as he continued towards the old woman. As he passed, the travellers parted to make way for him. Mike detected the mixture of fear, anger, and distaste they felt towards him. It was so powerful he could almost smell it, his senses on high alert after years of dealing with similar situations.

The old woman retreated inside her caravan, and Mike climbed the steps to the small entrance, twisting his shoulders sideways to get through the door. He looked around. Just as the outside of the old woman's caravan was in stark contrast to the rickety, scruffy, patched-together appearance of the camp, the inside was densely packed and cosy. The back half of the caravan was hidden behind a red and gold velvet curtain. It was a little threadbare in places but filled the caravan with a sense of luxury and mystery. The other half of the caravan was stuffed with leather-bound books that sat amongst elegant woodcarvings and brass instruments, which Mike could not fathom. Throws made from intricately patterned, colourful fabrics lay over almost every surface, and the air was filled with the aroma of warm cinnamon and cloves.

"Detective Inspector Mike Nicholls," the old woman said, the words tripping from her mouth like scattered pebbles. "Am I right?"

Mike stood upright as he always did when addressed and bumped his head on the wooden frame of the caravan. He pursed his lips but remained stoic, steadfastly refusing to rub the spot despite having given it a nasty crack. He turned to the woman, who now sat at the end of the caravan behind a round, mahogany table. "How do you know my name?"

"It's my job to know these things," she replied simply.

Mike squinted in the gloom. The woman's appearance was shocking. Her old, craggy face alluded to a hard life. Her hair was long, thick, and grey—a few locks braided, a few beaded—her puckered mouth a thin line. Above her rough, dark, leathery cheeks, two large, startlingly green, almond-shaped eyes stared at him. Mike suspected that the woman's reputation as a witch was predicated on those eyes. They opened wide as if everything in front of them was worthy of her acute attention, and the woman examined Mike as though he were a specimen in a jar.

"And what's your name?" he asked, determined to appear unimpressed by the fact she had known his.

"They call me Jonquil," the old woman said with a gap-toothed smile. "It is French for daffodil." Jonquil's missing teeth offered Mike a view into the black cavern of her mouth, and it occurred to him that she couldn't look less like a daffodil if she tried.

"Last name?"

The old woman laughed. Not quite a cackle, but close. She certainly played her part well.

"No need for another name when you live amongst family."

"I've heard you've a reputation as a witch?"

"What's a witch?" Jonquil asked playfully. "If a witch is a scorned woman, then yes, I am. Amongst your people, at least. Amongst my own, I am revered." She lifted her hands to frame her face, her bracelets jangling, large rings on every finger in a silver metal Mike couldn't identify.

He sighed loudly. "I'm not here to listen to riddles or witness a pantomime. I'm here because a woman has been murdered, and there are signs that the person who killed her believed her to be a witch. Now, your witchiness and presumable knowledge of, um, witchery and the fact that you and your fellows were recently moved on from the land near where the murder took place connects you to the death in ways that need looking at. It's in your interest to tell me anything you can that might help me."

Jonquil cast her big, twinkling green eyes up and down the inspector's frame, her wrinkled expression showing little sign of respect. "You're a good man," she said slowly.

"I'm a police officer."

Jonquil smiled. "The two are not the same thing, Inspector, believe me."

Mike looked at her. There was a slight note of regret in her big, expressive eyes. Suddenly he wondered if he had made a mistake in coming to the camp. Following the sacked farmhand lead might have been a better use of his time. "Look, if one woman was murdered because she was thought to be a witch, it's possible that you're in danger as well. What do you know of Kathleen Webster?"

"I have never heard the name," Jonquil said.

"She was the victim. Owner of Webster's Farm. Surely someone in your community encountered her when you camped on her land?"

"I know nothing, Inspector. I only see."

Mike pinched the bridge of his nose. "What do you see then?"

The change in Jonquil's face was remarkable. Her green irises disappeared as she closed her eyes and the wrinkles in her face faded. She lifted her ring-clad fingers in front of her, as if feeling her way through darkness. Mike's heart began to beat harder. The hair on the back of his neck, recently cut in preparation for the wedding and so sharp he could almost cut his hand on it, stood up on end. He felt like he was visiting some cheap seaside pier attraction, but nevertheless he watched the old woman with a mixture of confusion and alarm.

"I see . . . old conflicts reawakened on this land," Jonquil uttered in a low monotone. "I see . . . an evil entity performing under the guise of purity. I see . . . a clash between ancient, long-dormant forces . . ."

"You'll see an arrest warrant with your name on it if you're not very careful!" Mike snapped.

Jonquil shook her head and opened her eyes, her green irises flashing back into view again. She smiled at him. "Such scepticism."

"Look, I've already spoken to one blathering old lady today. Focus please, and answer my questions!"

Jonquil laughed. "Why do you ask so many, Inspector, when you lack the ability to listen to the answers?"

"Now look, I—"

He stopped as the woman's face relaxed again and she

fell into a trance-like state, her eyes closing, her hands raised in front of her like before. As Mike watched Jonquil, the gold leaf pattern in the curtain behind her leapt to life. The trefoils and stripes began to swirl, and he staggered, suddenly woozy and off-balance, clutching at his head and reaching out with his other arm to steady himself against a cabinet.

"You are in a heavenly place," Jonquil intoned. "Your chest high with pride, your eyes soft with anticipation. But your bride, she is not there. She's running away from you. Away . . . Her beautiful white dress trailing behind her . . . Others follow. But she is running . . . Faster . . . Running towards danger . . . "

Mike closed his eyes and saw dancing, brightly coloured lights spinning underneath his eyelids. Jonquil's words repeated themselves in his mind, gnawing away at his brain, accompanied by a whooshing sound. The lights spun faster before abruptly disappearing, and Mike opened his eyes to see the old woman smiling her unattractive smile in front of him. He took his hand from the cabinet and stood upright, defiant and aggrieved. Then he flinched as he banged his head again. He glared at the self-satisfied, smiling old woman as he struggled to recover and reassert his authority.

He pointed a shaking finger at her. "I'm not done with you," he said. "If I find out that you, or anyone in your camp, was involved in this murder, I will be coming back here to take in as many of you as is necessary. And I will regard this little . . . parlour trick as evidence of resistance. Do I make myself clear?"

Jonquil merely laughed, and still vexed, Mike stamped out of the caravan and down the steps, taking care to grip the handrail tightly. He marched through the congregation of contemptuous travellers who had assembled, this time to form a guard of dishonour. He ignored them as they glowered, chewed, and jeered, grateful now to the sharp wind for clearing his head.

CHAPTER SIXTEEN

FEW THINGS WERE as enjoyable to Annabelle as dinner with friends. The musical notes of cutlery clinking against plates, the ripple of laughter that followed shared jokes, the passing and sharing of plates, wine, sometimes babies—all enriched some deep part of her soul.

She was especially looking forward to tonight's dinner. On the guest list was her beloved Father John, her oldest friend Mary, and the rare company of Harper Jones. Mary's husband, Rafael, was arriving in a couple of days, as was Harper's. Mike's absence was a slight disappointment, but Annabelle wasn't going to worry too much about it. They had a lifetime to dine together.

Despite her excitement, there was an air of tension that loomed over the preparation of the meal as Annabelle and Philippa worked in the kitchen to ready the table and the food. Annabelle watched as Philippa practically threw the cutlery on the table. She winced and briefly closed her eyes as Philippa returned the roasting tin to the oven with a loud clatter and a slam of the glass door. She knew perfectly well what was causing Philippa to behave this way; she also knew she should break the tension by acknowledging Philippa's concerns. But with every bang and crash, Annabelle became increasingly reluctant to do so, and as the preparations went on, the fouler Philippa's mood became.

Finally, it was Philippa who waded into the breach. "I hope you had fun today," she snapped as she folded napkins like she was wrangling chickens.

"I beg your pardon."

"I said I hope you had fun—gallivanting about the village, snooping in nooks and crannies. You know, you'll have to give up those adventures of yours once you become a wife."

"What are you saying, Philippa? There was a murder! In our community, of a member of our community," Annabelle said, gesticulating wildly with red polka-dot oven-mitt-covered hands.

"Which is a matter for your future husband, not you! For a professional!"

"If there's any way in which I can help, I shall, Philippa! This affects my people. My flock."

"And even if you can't help, you'll stick your nose in!" Philippa said, looking away suddenly.

Annabelle gazed at her, the jug full of water, ice cubes, and sliced lemon that she held in her hand suspended in midair. She blinked quickly. "I see." Annabelle put the jug down carefully on the table.

"People are starting to gossip, Vicar."

"Starting?" Annabelle said. "When did they ever stop?" She raised her eyebrows and turned to look through the door of the oven, ostensibly to check on the beef Wellington that was to be their main course.

"They're saying that you've got cold feet. That you're having second thoughts. They say that you're struggling to . . . to . . . commit!"

Annabelle spun around and placed her hands on her hips. "What nonsense!"

"I wish I could tell them that." Philippa looked down at the tea towel she was twisting in her hands. "But even I'm not sure of it anymore." She looked up at Annabelle with big, doleful eyes.

"Philippa!" Annabelle said. "I love Mike; he loves me. We're going to be married in a few days, and that is that!"

"Then why won't you help me make this wedding the best it can be?" Philippa implored desperately. "You haven't even tried on your wedding dress!"

"Yes, I have! It's fine!"

"Are you sure about that?"

"I tried it on a month ago! You were there!"

"A month ago . . ." Philippa nodded sceptically. "And how many jam tarts and strawberry cupcakes have you had since then? You must have set a new record scoffing that jam roly-poly Mrs. Applebottom brought over last week. You hoovered it up like you were frightened it would escape. You had cream, ice cream, *and* custard with it!"

"What are you trying to say, Philippa?" Annabelle said, although she knew very well. She frowned.

Philippa, undeterred by the look on Annabelle's face, continued, "I'm just saying that you should at least try the dress on again this close to the wedding in case it needs altering. Otherwise, there's a danger there'll be gaping bits here and escaping bits there. You don't want to look like a sausage tied in ribbon in your wedding photos! They're forever, wedding photos are!"

"How rude!" Annabelle exclaimed.

Philippa sighed. Her shoulders slumped forwards. "I'm sorry, Vicar, but . . ."

"You don't sound very sorry!"

"I just want your wedding to be perfect—for your sake. Our sakes, the village's sake. I want to help you. I want to help make it the best day it can be. I want your wedding to be glorious and wonderful so you can look back on it for the rest of your life with a feeling of joy."

"I'm not one for fussing over my appearance; you know that, Philippa!"

"Oh, I understand, and that you don't care much for pomp and circumstance either, but ten years from now when you're looking at your wedding photos, celebrating your anniversaries, you'll thank me." Philippa blew out her cheeks. She sat down quickly and ran a hand over her brow. For her, her little speech had transgressed a number of rules she held herself to. Not being emotional, vulnerable, or desperate were three of them.

Annabelle's irritation melted in the face of Philippa's dejection. Before she could say anything, however, the doorbell rang.

CHAPTER SEVENTEEN

WITHOUT LOOKING AT the vicar, Philippa went to open the front door. There, beaming and carrying a bunch of carnations as pink as her cheeks, stood Annabelle's oldest friend and matron of honour, Mary, formerly Sister Mary, but now Mrs. Mary Durand. She looked as sweet and demure as ever. She was also currently nearly as wide as she was tall due to the advanced state of her pregnancy. Philippa privately thought that Mary threatened to eclipse even Annabelle in the wedding photos, should said wedding photos ever get taken.

Behind Mary stood Father John, his big frame sagging under the weight of a large crate he carried. He was keen to put it down, but the air filled with greetings, air kisses, the bangs and crashes of people entering, yelps from the dog, and directions to "Come on through!"

"Mary! How are you feeling? Everything going well?"

"Ooh! This is heavy!"

"It's terribly nippy out there!"

"Tell me where to put this, quick! My knees are going!"

Father John went ahead to put the crate down in a corner of the kitchen before being hugged by Annabelle and introduced to Philippa.

"I'm so glad you're here!" Annabelle said, clinging to Father John like he was her favourite teddy bear, which in a way he was. His soft bulk warmed and comforted her.

"Me too, Annabelle. Especially under these circumstances."

"What's in there?" Annabelle asked as she pulled away and looked at the crate the priest had brought in with him.

"Ah," Father John said, leaning down to pull off the top.

"Wine from Ville d'Eauloise!" Mary announced. "A gift for the wedding. From the people of the village with their very best wishes. And there's these." She held up a string of sausages. "Selwyn said Mike enjoyed these very much." She wrinkled her nose. "Can't imagine why. They're made from strips of a pig's stomach. The casing is made from its colon."

"Huh, well don't tell Mike that. He thought it was the tastiest sausage and chips he'd ever eaten." Annabelle pulled a wine bottle from the opened crate and inspected it. "How wonderful! Mind if we crack one open tonight to celebrate seeing you again?"

"Of course not!" Mary laughed.

"Are we early?" Father John asked as he hung his coat up.

"Only a little," Philippa said. "We're just waiting for Harper."

"Is Mike not coming?"

"Unfortunately not," Annabelle said as she held a bottle of wine with one hand and twisted the corkscrew with the other. "He's busy."

"With the investigation," Philippa said.

"Terrible business," Mary added.

"We're lucky that Annabelle is even here," Philippa added. Annabelle pressed her lips together and screwed up her face. Whether that was down to popping the cork or Philippa's words wasn't clear.

"How has your visit gone so far?" Annabelle said as she went to collect some glasses. "Is your accommodation comfortable? I'm so sorry I can't host you here, but as you can see, there's no room at the inn."

"Oh, Annabelle." Mary sighed happily. "The whole village seems to be alive with excitement over your wedding!"

"Everywhere I've been, it's the first topic of conversation. Even that chap who showed me the way to the village wanted to know all about it," Father John said. Annabelle handed him a glass of wine, her hand shaking slightly.

"I can almost taste the energy!" Mary said. "It's going to be such a day. I can't wait. Oh, no wine for me, Annabelle. Thank you, though." She rubbed her big, round, pregnant belly proudly.

"It was all people were talking about in the pub," Father John continued. "I took a short side visit to the Dog and Duck before I got here," he explained. "Nice little pub. I've heard so much about Cornish beers from the real ale enthusiasts in my congregation. I promised them that I would try them all out and report back. On their behalf of course," he added in response to Annabelle's raised eyebrows. "Katie Flynn said almost every available room in the village is taken up with one guest or another. I hear villagers have even been offering up their spare rooms! What a wonderful community you've built here, Annabelle. Can you fit everyone into the church?"

Annabelle didn't reply. She'd abruptly turned back to

check on the beef Wellington. There was an awkward pause. The doorbell rang again.

"That must be Harper," Annabelle said, going to answer the door. "By the way, the victim at the farm today was her aunt. Just so you know."

Harper looked ravishing. She had pulled her black hair into an easy but elegant style that exposed the dramatic sparkling earrings that dangled from her ears. They coordinated with the necklace sitting at the base of her long neck. Her dress picked up the green in her hazel eyes and a little makeup accentuated her exotic features. Harper was striking enough in her work clothes; dressed up, she was truly magnetic. Annabelle drooped a little when she saw her.

"Everyone! This is Harper Jones, our local pathologist. She's helping with the case at the farm."

"Good evening. I'm very happy to be here and to meet you all."

"Hello, I'm Mary, Annabelle's oldest friend. I'm so sorry to hear about your aunt," Mary said. "Annabelle just told us."

"Thank you. Please don't feel uncomfortable though. I am glad to be here." Harper gave a dazzling smile to confirm her words. She was, truly, glad to be there. An evening on her own had not appealed.

Annabelle introduced Philippa and reminded her that Father John had been at the farm earlier. Philippa murmured her condolences, and Annabelle offered Harper some wine, which she gratefully accepted. In her gracious and compassionate way, Annabelle steered the conversation away from weddings and deaths by enquiring about Mary's birth plans and Father John's inner city parish work, quietly smoothing over what might have been a difficult social situation until Philippa announced dinner was ready. "Now let's sit and eat!" Annabelle cried, steering them all to the table.

CHAPTER EIGHTEEN

PHILIPPA SERVED CREAM of broccoli soup as a starter. The broccoli had come from Albert Bostwick's allotment, whilst the cream had been siphoned off the top of the milk from Leo Tremethick's cows. Less endearingly, the stock that formed the base of the soup had been contributed by one of Alma Whittell's older chickens. With everyone but Mary already in thrall to the magnificent French wine, the conversation flowed quickly and smoothly. For the first time in a while, Annabelle found herself relaxing, the tension in her shoulders and the shadowy thoughts that lurked at the back of her mind melting amidst the warmth of the food, atmosphere, and people around her.

"Who did you meet when you were in the pub?" Annabelle said to Father John during a momentary lull in the conversation.

John swallowed the last of his soup. "So many people; such a friendly place. When they heard I was officiating your wedding, no one would let me buy anything! I also met that Samuel Bellingham again. Terribly nice chap."

"Who's Samuel Bellingham?" asked Mary. Philippa began clearing the starter whilst Annabelle prepared to bring the main course to the table.

"A historian," answered Father John. "I met him at the murder scene earlier. Oh, I apologise, Harper."

"It's alright, Father John," Harper said.

"What was he doing there?" exclaimed Mary in surprise.

"The same as the rest of the crowd," Harper said drily. "Craning their necks. Half the village seemed to be there."

"We ended up talking about the paganism that existed in this area long ago, particularly witchcraft."

"Witchcraft!" Mary laughed. "Why-ever would you talk about that?"

"There were similarities between my aunt's murder and those of so-called witches back in the day," Harper said, shrugging her shoulders. Mary's eyes widened as her small, neat mouth formed a perfect O, perfectly complementing her big round belly. It seemed that she was all curves and circles. There was nothing about her that was angular at all. Philippa brought the beef Wellington to the table.

"Oh, that looks as good as it smells!" Father John said, leaning over to inhale the sweet, meaty aroma as Philippa placed the platter on the table. "And I bet it's going to taste even better."

"Don't get distracted now." Annabelle smiled as Philippa began to slice the meat in front of them. "Carry on with what you were saying." As Father John talked, Annabelle quietly took a middle piece of beef for Mike. It was important she do it now. Smelling as good as it did, it was unlikely there would be anything left of it at the end.

"Well," Father John said, struggling to pick up the

thread of his thoughts as he gazed covetously at the meat pasted with pâté, rolled in thinly sliced ham, and wrapped in a coat of glossy, moist, slightly brown, flaky pastry. "He was telling me about witch-finders of old. How they would hound these poor women and isolate them by creating a fervour against them in the community. There was one in particular . . . Oh, what was his name . . . Hopkins! Witchfinder Hopkins! Terrible fellow. Quite famous in his day, apparently."

"What did he do?" Philippa asked, passing a plate of the beef to him.

"This Hopkins chap would move from town to town in search of so-called witches. He must have been very charismatic, because despite having the flimsiest of credentials, he managed to galvanise whole communities into following him. Some of his supporters were devout, fanatical even."

"Sounds like a cult," Harper said.

"Indeed." Father John quickly sliced off a chunk of meat and pastry and munched it, closing his eyes blissfully as the others waited for him to continue his story.

"But how did he know the women were witches?" Mary asked.

"He was particularly crafty when it came to that. He would look for what he called 'devil's marks.' A wart, a mole, even a flea-bite could be interpreted as a sign that a woman was a witch."

"But they're so common!" Mary said, horrified. "I've got more than one." They all looked at her dubiously.

"I can recommend a cream for that, Mary," Annabelle said, patting her hand. "Or this special kind of spray."

"Oh, I didn't mean . . . Moles, I meant moles, everyone." They all relaxed, and Father John carried on.

"Precisely," he said. "We'd all be witches if that were the criteria." John took a sip of wine. "He particularly targeted women who gave birth to girls. After the drink with Samuel, I spent over an hour reading about witch-finders online. Hopkins would use all manner of tricks to convince his followers that the women he targeted were evil with special powers. Here, let me show you."

Father John looked around, searching the kitchen before finding what he wanted—a toothpick. He plucked one from its small container, then addressed Mary.

"Where do you have a mole?"

Suddenly fearful, Mary gulped. "O-on my arm?"

"Give me your arm then."

"It won't hurt, will it? The baby . . ."

"No, no, it won't hurt. And your baby will be absolutely fine."

"Go on!" Philippa urged excitedly. Her mood had lifted like a balloon as Father John had told his story. "This is more entertaining than bingo!"

Tentatively, her smile quivering beneath wide eyes, Mary offered her arm to Father John, pulling up her sleeve to reveal a mole.

"Perfect!" Father John said, holding Mary's arm in one hand and the toothpick in the other, "Now, imagine this toothpick is a three-inch needle."

"Oh my! I'm going to faint!" Mary gasped.

"If Mary is a witch, and this mole before you really is a devil's mark according to Hopkins, then I should be able to press this entire toothpick into it without Mary feeling anything more than a slight prick."

Annabelle gasped. Mary's eyes widened even further. Philippa smiled like a self-satisfied cat, as if she were witnessing the great Houdini.

"Are you sure this is safe?" Harper asked.

"Safer than having dinner with a witch," Father John said, now fully embodying his role as the evening's entertainer. He flourished the toothpick in the air like a magician before gazing at the mole on Mary's arm. Four pairs of eyes focused like spotlights, long having forgotten the dinner on their plates as they waited for the moment of revelation to come.

"Tell me as soon as you feel pain, Mary."

"O-okay," Mary stuttered.

With the slow, suspenseful pace of a showman, Father John glanced up one last time, then brought the toothpick to the mole. There were a few clipped gasps around the table, then everyone held their breath. Father John pressed the toothpick to Mary's skin, and it began to disappear. He continued pressing, the toothpick easing into Mary as smoothly as a pole into the calmest of water. It was undeniable.

"Mary!" Annabelle cried in astonishment. "Doesn't it hurt?"

"No!" the former nun cried.

"But it's going in!"

"I know!"

"Sanguis Christi, inebria me!" Mary yelped.

Father John's audience exchanged frightened glances. Skin turned pale, jaws were clenched. Biscuit entered the room and immediately left again.

"It doesn't hurt!" cried Mary, unsure whether to be panic-stricken or triumphant.

When they could no longer see any part of the thin, tiny wooden stick, Father John pulled his hand away with a dramatic, elaborate flourish. Frantically, the others leant forwards to scrutinise Mary's bare arm, their minds spinning as they sought some explanation. Father John waved his palm over the remains of the beef Wellington before turning it over to show those seated around the table.

CHAPTER NINETEEN

THERE, IN FATHER John's hand, lay the toothpick. It was not embedded in Mary's skin. "As I pressed, I simply pushed it back into my hand, concealing it from your view," he explained. It took a second, but when the realisation hit, the palpable tension in the room relaxed, akin to a massive rainstorm after days of mugginess.

"Heavens!" Annabelle said, clasping at her thumping heart. Mary giggled nervously as all her fear escaped in a rush. Philippa clapped happily.

Harper sat back, smiling faintly. "Bravo! Bravo! Father John, you are wasted as a priest!"

Once the laughter had eased their nerves and colour had returned to their faces, Annabelle said, "How dreadful! To condemn women to death on the basis of some silly magic trick!"

"That wasn't all," Father John said, smiling with satisfaction at the success of his performance. "Another trick was to ask a woman to recite the Lord's Prayer—something an embarrassing amount of my parish still can't do. If the woman made a mistake, he would take that as a sign of being a witch."

"And if they recited it perfectly?" Mary asked.

"He would say it was a trick of the devil and still condemn them."

"How awful!"

"He sounds like a psychopath enabled and supported by the gullible and unpleasant," Harper said crisply as she returned to her food.

"You're not wrong there," Father John said. "Hopkins was a nasty piece of work and preyed on the sanctimonious and the poorly educated, which was almost everyone in those days. The Church didn't come up smelling of roses either. Too many priests were willing to turn a blind eye or even support the practice. Thousands of women were put to death in awful circumstances over nothing but ignorance and prejudice."

"Harper!" Annabelle said, waving at the woman at the other end of the table. "You didn't forget the book, did you?"

"No!" Harper said, putting her knife and fork down. "I have it right here."

"What book?" Philippa asked as Harper reached into her bag.

"We found a book in my aunt's room. It seemed peculiar, but neither Annabelle nor I could make heads nor tails of it. Annabelle thought Father John might have some insight."

Father John sneaked one more bite of beef and pastry into his mouth before abandoning his knife and fork once again. "Let me have a look."

Harper took the book from the paper she had wrapped it in and carefully handed it to the priest. She sat back and sipped her wine as she waited patiently for his thoughts.

"What do you think?" Annabelle asked a few seconds later, not quite so patiently.

"It's a very interesting specimen," Father John said as he turned the book in his hands. "It's well covered, but essentially made of cardboard, so the owner can't have been made of money. It's certainly been through a bit of a bashing. The method of binding is strong..."

"Written by one Martha B. George. It says '1857' on the cover. In the corner," Annabelle said.

Father John carefully opened the book. "Oh yes, the date is accurate. The hue of the ink, the feel of the paper. Definitely mid-1800s."

"You can tell that much from ink?" Philippa asked.

"It's rather amusing to think that if I spill a little water on my ballpoint-written sermon notes, they'll be ruined, yet two hundred or so years ago, they were using inks that have lasted centuries," Father John said. "And yet we still insist we've made progress."

"Can you make anything of the writing?" Harper said.

"Let's see," Father John replied. He delicately flicked through the pages. "Presumably you noticed that it was some kind of diary."

Annabelle gathered up a final forkful of peas and beef before setting her knife and fork side by side on her plate. "Go on," she said.

"It seems to be some sort of travel journal . . ." Father John said slowly as he squinted at the flowing script. "It's rather difficult to understand. Old-ee English-ee. And some misspellings. She writes about 'Cornovii.' Is that some kind of old name for Cornwall?"

"No," Annabelle said, suddenly alert. "That's probably a reference to the ancient Cornovii tribe who lived here. This region takes their name from them, so the story goes, or maybe it was the other way around. We're talking Iron Age."

"Just imagine all those people, warriors, and families marching through the countryside, building villages, organising themselves into communities—all for a better life. Pilgrims of a kind," Mary said dreamily.

"I doubt it was very romantic. Full of fear, starvation, desperation, and physical hardship, I should imagine. They were warriors alright," Harper said. "Fighting people. Fighting for their lives, peace, and safety, but not afraid to defend themselves to the death if they had to. It was survival of the fittest back in 500 AD."

The others ate slowly as Father John leafed through the dusty book. "There's reference here to a daughter," he said. "Seems these words are being written by a young woman who is taking her baby somewhere."

"How interesting," Mary said.

"Hmmm . . ." Father John trailed off, his countenance darkening. He put one hand to the back of his neck. The clanging of cutlery stopped as the others in the room watched him, his eyes fixed upon the book in horror. He reached out to pick up his wine and slowly raised his glass to his lips, his hand trembling as he gulped the wine down with one swig.

"What is it?" Harper asked.

"Father John?" Annabelle said. "Are you alright?"

"There's . . . There's . . ." He pointed his finger at the page, his face pale as he looked across at them. "It mentions Hopkins."

CHAPTER TWENTY

"THE WITCH-FINDER?" HARPER said after a second's pause. Father John nodded.

"Read it," Annabelle said brusquely.

"Oh no, don't!" Mary argued. "I've had enough frights tonight already!" Annabelle reached out a hand to comfort her.

"It could be important," Harper said. "If my aunt was killed because someone thought she was a witch and she had in her possession a book that mentioned those who hunted witches, albeit many, many years ago, it's a connection the police can't ignore."

"But the book was written a hundred, what, a hundred and fifty years ago!" Philippa said.

"And witches don't exist," argued Annabelle. "But perhaps Kathleen's murderer doesn't agree."

"Go on," Harper said.

Father John looked up at Mary for confirmation that she didn't mind him continuing. As fascinated as the rest, she nodded, and the priest returned to the large but beautiful handwritten words on the page.

"'Today's dawn was lifted by angels, no eye but pure deserved to receive. Though I might steal it, I have not dared, for in the east, Edward Butterworth resides. He is that man of Hopkins, wrought from anger and hatred into a beast with blackened blood . . .'"

Father John ran his finger down the page.

"'For he that claims I am more than mere woman, that my babe is more than mere ungrown flesh and mind, is one who makes animals of us both with this feral pursuit.'"

It was Philippa who broke the silence that hung heavy in the air when Father John paused. "I didn't understand a word of that," she said flatly. If she expected a laugh, she was disappointed. The dark, oppressive mood remained.

"It sounds like she was being chased by a man called Edward Butterworth," Harper explained. "And that he was a follower of Matthew Hopkins."

"Because he thought she was a witch," Mary added. "'More than mere woman'—that must be what it means, no?"

"Yes, I think that's what it means. Edward Butterworth thought she was a witch, and her baby too," Annabelle said.

"I see," Philippa replied, her mood as dark now as those around her.

"Listen to this," Father John said, still transfixed by the book.

"'Consideration has long since brought me to the truth of the matter. My husband, the betrayer. As hammer to nail, he drove Butterworth to me. Gave him scent and unbound collar to hunt me.'"

Father John paused again. Harper explained for Philippa. "She thinks her husband put Butterworth onto her and perhaps gave him means to find her."

"Pah!" Philippa exclaimed. "Men! They're as crafty getting rid of you as they are trying to win you over." The others didn't laugh, and a dark cloud continued to hang over the meal.

"Did you mention this to the inspector?" Father John asked.

"No," Harper said.

"He has very little time for superstitions," Annabelle explained. "Besides, he'll say that it was centuries ago and of no relevance."

"Still," Father John said, "I think we should mention it to him." He turned to Harper. "Do you mind if I keep this a while? I could try to decipher as much of it as possible. It might prove useful."

"Of course," Harper said. "You're the only person who seems to be able to make any sense of it. Here, I'll wrap it in the paper for you."

"Excellent," Father John said. "How can I get hold of you?"

"I'm staying at Mrs. Sutton's B and B until after the wedding," Harper replied.

"I'm a few houses down, above the lovely tea shop, Flynn's. Such a wonderful aroma in the mornings! I'll let you know if I find anything interesting."

"Wonderful. I'll keep digging from my end too. I'm keen to know how, and why, my aunt came to own this book. Perhaps Martha George settled in the area," Harper said.

"That sounds like a good idea to me." Father John picked up his knife and fork again. As he cut into his beef

Wellington, he looked over at Annabelle. "You know, I can see why this sort of thing gets you so excited at times."

"What sort of thing?"

"This murder mystery thing?"

"All part of a country vicar's daily duties, Father. It's important that justice is served. It's the only way the community feels safe. I simply wish it wouldn't happen quite so often in these parts."

"Please," Mary said. "Can we change the subject from murders and witches and horrible men who chase innocent women across the country? My little one is protesting." They all looked at her bump, which they could see quite clearly because Mary sat two feet from the table. Her arms couldn't reach. Philippa had cut up her food and Mary was forced to balance her plate on her bump and eat her dinner with a fork. As they watched, her belly morphed from a perfect round to one with a corner in the middle of it. "Oof. See?" Mary said.

"Of course." Father John chuckled lightly. "We haven't even talked about the reason we're all here—your wedding, Annabelle!"

"Oh yes!" Mary said, brightening. "You must show me your dress, Annabelle. Would you wear it for me after dinner?"

"The question is could she," Philippa muttered from behind her wine glass. Annabelle glared at her.

"Have you written your vows yet?" Harper asked.

"More to the point, have you written Mike's?" Father John joked.

"Who's Mike's best man?"

"How soon will we see the photographs?"

"What's your bouquet going to be like?"

"Which hymns have you chosen?"

"Are you having live music at the reception?"

"Will you put cans on the back of your going away car? Oh, I do hope you have cans!"

"Have you two decided where you're going to live afterwards?"

Annabelle put on a brave smile as she was bombarded with questions, none of which she could answer adequately. She felt uncomfortable, but worse was the dread that crept over her as she realised that she preferred the subject of murder and witch hunts to that of her own wedding.

CHAPTER TWENTY-ONE

ANNABELLE USUALLY SLEPT deeply and easily, and after her hectic day, the big meal, several glasses of wine, and fielding endless questions about her wedding, she was virtually comatose when she put her head on her pillow that night.

But the activities of the day, her joy at seeing old friends, and the subsequent exhaustion couldn't stop her dreaming frightful nightmares. They flitted through her unconscious mind in disturbing vignettes as she struggled, tossing and groaning with frustration, amongst the sheets on her bed. In one dream, she stood at the doors of the church, Mike waiting, familiar faces all turned towards her smiling expectantly. Her father was beside her, their arms locked. For a moment, her heart swelled with joy and happiness, but when she tried to walk down the aisle with him, her entire body seemed encased in concrete. Her dress was too tight, her body immobile. She could barely move her head. As everyone in the church waited for her to make her way to the altar, her betrothed, and their married future, Annabelle was stuck. The atmosphere soured, and

Annabelle felt overwhelmed with embarrassment and failure.

In another, she ran across grassy fields, chased by some shadowy, terrifying figure. She ran until she was near the Webster smallholding, glancing frantically behind her as the shadow drew closer. She ran into the barn, but immediately realised that there was nowhere to go. She spun around so that the shadowy figure was in front of her, big and tall. It gripped a pitchfork, an evil, satisfied grin on its face as it lunged forwards. Annabelle twisted and turned, hands tight around the pitchfork's shaft, the thing screaming all the while . . .

"Vicar! Annabelle! You're going to take my arm clean off!"

Annabelle awoke with a start. It took a second, but the looming, powerful shadow revealed itself to be Philippa, and the pitchfork that Annabelle tightly clutched Philippa's slight, sinewy forearm.

"Oh!" Annabelle called out, letting go.

Philippa straightened up and rubbed her arm. "Goodness me, you're not always this awful before your first tea of the morning, Reverend! What is going on?"

"Philippa! I'm so sorry!" Annabelle said, sitting up against the headboard and putting her hand to her brow in shock. She closed her eyes and took deep breaths. "What happened?"

"I came to wake you, and the next thing I knew you were yanking my arm like a madwoman!"

"I was having a dreadful nightmare."

Philippa sighed. The pain in her arm lessened and she stopped rubbing it to look at the vicar. "I'm afraid your nightmare has only just begun."

"What?"

"Something terrible has happened." Philippa looked away, pressing her lips together and rolling them over her teeth as she thought of what to say. "I've just got off the phone with Sophie at Woodlands Manor. The marquee for your wedding reception . . ."

"Yes?"

"Someone has burned it down."

CHAPTER TWENTY-TWO

IT WAS PHILIPPA'S turn to grasp the dashboard as Annabelle's Mini Cooper tilted first this way, then that. It powered through the country lanes, its wheels screeching like an agitated monkey, the motor roaring like an angry lion. Typically, Philippa enjoyed taking an exhilarating ride through the countryside with Annabelle as her driver. It was a bit like taking part in a road race—thrilling. But this morning, Annabelle's speed was fuelled by shock and anxiety.

In record time, they reached the thick forest of oaks that hid the splendour of Woodlands Manor from view. The magnificent, palatial estate had been owned by Gabriella and Sophie for a while now—two sassy, quick-witted former London socialites who gave up their fashionable lifestyles for the old-world extravagance of a country mansion. Under their shrewd, tasteful management, the large property had been transformed into a luxurious resort boasting all manner of services and a refuge for the pampered and the curious.

In addition to relaxing in the huge, striking bedrooms

and palatial bathrooms, guests could partake of healthy, delicious food prepared by the finest chefs enticed by Sophie and Gabriella from their favourite restaurants in London. Distractions and treatments designed to aid recovery from the stresses of a busy life presented themselves in the form of masseuses, beauticians, and healers. Patrons of the spa could pop into the converted servants' quarters for a swim, a sauna, or even a mud bath. Active types loved the tennis courts, horse trekking, and clay pigeon shooting, whilst the more adventurous lavished praise on the regular events held at the estate. There were murder-mystery evenings, masked balls, scavenger hunts, and even escape rooms for those who loved to solve puzzles.

Woodlands Manor had also become a hotspot for period drama productions. Producers sought out the property for its historically authentic architecture and well-preserved features, whilst Gabriella and Sophie played host to numerous ghost hunters who regularly booked nights during the quieter, dark winter months in search of apparitions that were rumoured to haunt the house.

There was never any question that Annabelle's wedding reception would be held there, least of all because the vicar had played an integral role in the transformation of Woodlands Manor from private estate to destination resort, employer, and boon to the local economy. Annabelle had been tireless as she'd advocated, lobbied, recommended, and suggested. "How about breakfasts with eggs from Mrs. Whittell's chickens? They're simply delicious." "Oscar Beardsley's an excellent painter and decorator." "Morwenna Mumford's daughter's looking for a job. She'd make a good receptionist." "Have you considered reenactment weekends? Chadwick Bushnell is really into that." Oh yes, Sophie and Gabriella had plans, great plans, for Annabelle's wedding. Plans that Annabelle hadn't quite been able to throw herself into. And perhaps now wouldn't be able to.

After a minute of driving through trees, the dense woods ended. In front of Annabelle and Philippa, the impressive house and grounds emerged like a mirage. A grand vista loomed: an enormous, finely architected, elegant country house surrounded by immaculately tended lawns, budding flowers, and stone balustrades. The view regularly drew gasps and murmurs of awe, but this time there were none. Annabelle's and Philippa's eyes were immediately drawn to the blackened mass which lay like a vast burnt-out parachute on the grass in front of the big house.

Annabelle parked hastily, barely registering Mike's car nearby. She got out in a flurry. She ran over to the remnants of the marquee's burned canvas that lay on the lawn. Wisps of smoke curled into the air, and an acrid smell made her recoil. Mike stood beside the two spa owners: tall, slim Gabriella, elegant from her sapphire-blue eyes to her high-heeled feet, and the darker, enigmatic Sophie, catlike and alluring. All three gawped at the devastation on the ground, the women silent for once. Annabelle rushed to the inspector's side, clutching his arm. Philippa caught up a second later.

"Crikey!" Annabelle exclaimed. "What happened?"

"Looks like a fire caught hold. I just got here myself," Mike said, extending a comforting arm around Annabelle's shoulders before turning to the two owners of the spa. "What do you know about this?"

"Less than you, most likely," Sophie said.

"Guests from our early morning yoga class alerted us," Gabriella added.

"Not a pleasant thing to wake up to."

"Certainly not."

Gabriella and Sophie had, over many years of knowing one another, acquired an uncommon ability to converse as one. They were in the habit of finishing each other's sentences. They would carry on a conversation whilst excluding any other party present, demoting them to mere bystanders in their singsongy back-and-forth performances. Mike sighed and rubbed Annabelle's shoulder before she stepped forwards to more closely inspect the remains.

"When was the marquee put up?" Mike asked.

"Yesterday," Sophie said.

"No, the night before," Gabriella corrected.

"Oh yes. It was here when we got up yesterday."

"Our handyman spent half the night getting it just right."

"He'll be devastated."

"Absolutely."

"How long will it take to clear up this little mess?" Mike nodded over to the giant burnt marshmallow of a former tent.

"A day or so," Sophie said.

"To remove it and build a new one," Gabriella added.

"There's time, then?" Annabelle asked.

"The grass will take a while to recover."

"But yes, don't worry. Things'll be as good as new."

"You won't even know this happened."

Philippa stood fidgeting as she struggled to accept the scene before her. "I don't understand."

"What is there to understand?" Gabriella said.

"The thing's burnt to a crisp!" Sophie added.

"But how?" Philippa asked. "It can't have set itself alight!"

"Is there a chance something could have accidentally

set it on fire? A discarded cigarette? A firework, perhaps?" Mike asked.

"Oh no! The grass is pleasantly moist, it's far too early in the year for fireworks, and we don't allow smoking or anything like that. We are a health spa."

"People come here to get away from that sort of thing."

"The only smoking our guests are interested in is the smoked salmon."

Annabelle turned to Mike. "You don't think . . . Could this be . . . Is this is a message . . . for us?"

CHAPTER TWENTY-THREE

MIKE PURSED HIS lips. "I shouldn't think so. Is there anyone in your past who would oppose our marriage? Should I be worried about someone standing up at the ceremony and objecting?" He chuckled.

"No," Annabelle said. "Should I?" Mike opened his mouth but quickly closed it again.

Philippa gasped. She pointed to the middle of the charred debris. Following the direction of her finger, Annabelle tiptoed her way through the blackened grass and picked something up off the ground. Immediately, her hand flew to her mouth. She came back carrying a sliver of paper between her fingertips.

"There's something here!" she said, handing the scrap to Mike quickly.

Mike turned it in his hand. Large capital letters were scrawled on the paper, black ash obscuring part of it but leaving it mostly legible.

"What does it say?" Philippa asked.

Mike looked up reluctantly as he considered what he

should tell them. "'No dwelling shall hide the woman from her own evil,'" he said carefully.

"Oh my!" Sophie said, exchanging a look with Gabriella.

"Are they referring to us?" Gabriella wondered.

"They have to be!" Sophie responded.

"I can't imagine why someone would think us evil."

"They're referring to me! I'm the one getting married here!" Annabelle exclaimed. She looked at Mike for some sort of answer, some confirmation, but the inspector was lost in his own thoughts, still staring at the note in his hand as he stroked his chin.

"It's a strange message," he said. "It sounds like religious talk. Evil. Dwelling. You don't hear those words often these days." Annabelle sighed.

"Maybe he means the witch," Philippa offered. "Maybe it's something to do with the murder."

Mike looked at her, considering her words slowly. He thought of the question Jonquil had posed to him in her caravan. Was a witch just another term for a scorned woman? As much as he had tried to forget the travellers, and Jonquil in particular, her words came back to him.

"The farmhand," Annabelle said, breaking the silence. Her tone was harsher and more unforgiving than Mike had ever heard. "The one Joan mentioned. Neil. She said he had been complaining about 'some wedding or other.'"

Trying to soothe her nerves, Mike said, "Now hold on, we don't—"

Annabelle cut him off. "Do you know anyone called Neil, Sophie? Gabriella?"

"Neil, with the blond hair?" Gabriella said.

"I wouldn't say we knew him exactly," Sophie added.

"We hired him a week last Wednesday."

"And sacked him the same day."

Annabelle rubbed her chin. "Why?"

"Well," Gabriella said with the slow, dramatic tone of someone about to tell a story. "We put word out that we needed a little extra gardening help."

"And this young man showed up on our doorstep."

"Rather attractive, somewhat scruffy, but that only adds to your credentials when you're a gardener."

"He seemed very nice at first."

"Humble, charming."

"A little shy, very eager."

"So we introduced him to our head gardener and away they went."

"His first task was to pull up some weeds. Nothing particularly complex."

"Except the lad couldn't tell the difference between a dandelion and a dahlia."

"He'd pulled up half the flowerbed by the time our gardener checked on him."

"And swiftly gave him the heave-ho."

Mike looked at Annabelle. She was downcast.

"Oh! That's not all," Sophie continued. "Our Neil has been undertaking a grand tour of local employers, it seems."

"I don't understand," Mike said, struggling to keep up with the back-and-forth.

"We were in Katie Flynn's tea shop a few days ago."

"Fantastic selection that day."

"Quite excellent."

"Well, apparently Katie had also been recently acquainted with Neil's 'talents.' She hired him for her new delivery service."

"She'd been toying with the idea for months, and when

our young friend approached her about the job, she, like us, was charmed into hiring him."

"He made a grand total of two deliveries."

"The first one arrived at its destination, albeit in an unrecognisable, mushy pulp."

"The second was left on Garry Flintcroft's doorstep."

"When it was intended for Larry Flintoff!"

"He'd got the wrong address."

"And half the cakes were missing."

"Oh! Tell them about Barbara!"

"Ah! Barbara, yes! The Dog and Duck."

"Charming pub."

"She was looking for a replacement for Isolde—you know, the girl behind the bar. She's gone to Spain to teach English."

"Stunning girl."

"Oh yes. A waste going abroad with looks like that. Some dark, handsome boy will pick her up. She'll be lost to us."

"She could so easily marry money."

"Anyway, Neil turns up, has an interview, and Barbara is utterly taken with him."

"Stop us if you've heard this one before."

Annabelle and Mike knew it would be futile to protest and politely urged them on; Mike mostly to get it over with.

"At the end of the interview, Barbara asks him to pour a pint, you know, to test his ability to handle a pump."

"Oh, he pumped it alright!"

"Pumped it all over the floor!"

"The silly man held the glass under one spout and pulled the handle of another!"

"Nightmare."

Mike scratched his head. "Hold on. So this Neil is

looking for work all about the village, and he's obviously incompetent, but did he mention anything about the wedding to you? That's what I'm interested in."

Sophie thought for a second, then shook her head. "He didn't talk about a wedding to me."

"Nor to me."

"So apart from being completely useless," Mike said, "there's nothing about this Neil that would incriminate him directly." He gestured over to the charred mess on the lawn.

"He sounds too inept to burn down a marquee," Philippa added.

"There was nothing odd about him at all?" Annabelle asked.

"Well..."

CHAPTER TWENTY-FOUR

"**H**E WAS VERY religious."
"Deeply devout."
"Even had a little Bible in his coat pocket."
"Oh yes!"
"It was part of his charm, in a way."
"Indicated a trustworthy character."
"To us at least."

Annabelle sighed. "So, he could very well have written that note? Using words like 'evil' and 'dwelling'?" she said.

Sophie and Gabriella shrugged in unison. "Maybe so."

"If we find him, we can compare his handwriting with this note to prove he wrote it," Mike said.

"Where's this lad from?" Philippa demanded, suddenly taking charge. "I've never heard of this 'Neil' before. He must be new to the village."

"He was, I think," Gabriella said, looking at her companion.

Sophie squinted as she parsed her thoughts. "I asked him, but all he said was that he came from a . . . What was it?"

"Den of sin." Gabriella dropped her voice, her chin dimpling as she pressed her lips together.

"He talked like that sometimes. It was a bit strange."

Annabelle shot Mike a look. "Do you know where he lives?" Mike asked.

"No idea."

"Probably sleeping rough."

"Oh yes. The way he dressed."

"Very tatty."

"But Barbara said he tidied up for his short—"

"Very short."

"—stint at the pub."

After a moment of contemplation, during which all of them took another long, sorry look at the remnants of the marquee, Mike turned to the women and said, "Okay, ladies. Thank you for your help. That's all I need from you for now. I'll take it from here."

"Of course, Inspector."

"Don't worry about this," Sophie said. "We'll fix it up."

"You won't remember anything about it when your special day comes."

"We're so excited, aren't we, Gabriella, darling?"

"We have such plans, darling, *such* plans."

Mike nodded uncertainly, refraining from saying anything in case he set the women off again. Listening to them was like watching a couple ballroom dance whilst wrestling one another for the lead.

As he and Annabelle walked arm in arm back to their cars, Mike heaved a heavy sigh.

"I must say I'm very worried, Mike," Annabelle said when they were out of earshot of the two women.

"Me too!" Philippa added from behind.

Mike closed his eyes briefly. When he opened them, he

looked into his future wife's eyes and saw fear there. He felt a deep desire to protect Annabelle. It was easy to forget that despite her position in the local community and her determination and forthrightness in the face of challenges, Annabelle could be vulnerable.

"Here." He took her in a tight embrace. "It'll be alright on the night," he said quietly into her ear. He felt Annabelle relax. There was a long exhale and, glancing aside, he saw Philippa, who seemed as comforted by their hug as Annabelle. Showing a discretion for which she wasn't known, Philippa excused herself and went to sit in the car.

After a few more seconds, the couple parted, Annabelle managing a wobbly smile. Mike kissed her tenderly, allowing her a moment to compose herself. "I won't lie to you, Annabelle. It does seem like there might be trouble abroad."

"I don't understand," Annabelle said, shaking her head as she tried to order the events in a way that made sense. "All of this. The marquee. Kathleen Webster. It has to be this Neil person. He's at the root of it, I'm sure!"

"Come on now, Annabelle," Mike said. "This isn't like you. You don't normally jump to conclusions. That's my job."

"I know it!" Annabelle said.

"You normally accuse me of getting ahead of myself and here you are doing it. Let's go home and have a nice cup of sugary tea, maybe a biscuit or two.

But Annabelle was having none of it. "Have I ever been wrong about such things before?"

For a few seconds, Mike genuinely struggled to dispute this. "Well, there's a first time for everything" was all he could muster.

"It's clear what's happening," she said firmly. "This

Neil is a twisted character who fancies himself as some sort of witch-hunter, and he thinks I'm one of them."

Mike was aghast. "What, a witch? You?"

Annabelle nodded vigorously.

"That's a big leap of logic, Annabelle."

"Is it? Sophie and Gabriella talked about how deeply, obsessively religious he is. He's probably on a mission to seek out witches whom he sees as despicable, debauched sinners."

Mike laughed, then stopped abruptly when he saw Annabelle was serious. "But you're religious too! A member of the church. One with an official role. You are the very opposite of a witch. Why is he burning down your wedding marquee when you're on the same side? What reason could he have?"

"That I'm a woman priest? Lots of people don't agree with it, you know. They think we should have subservient roles, not leadership ones. Look, Neil gets hired here and there, then gets sacked. He was hired at the Websters' smallholding and gets sacked again. Then Kathleen is murdered. In the manner of a witch, I may add. The next thing you know the marquee is burned down—just as witches were once burned at the stake—and he even leaves a message behind that is clearly directed at me. We should put a guard on Katie Flynn's tea shop right away. The cake's probably next!"

Mike shook his head slowly. "That doesn't work for me as a theory. To go from cold-blooded murder to burning down a marquee is a big downgrade."

"Maybe it's a warning. There's worse to come," Philippa piped up from the car. Mike ignored her.

"Plus, we know nothing about this Neil apart from the fact he's utterly useless at anything he turns his attention to.

That doesn't sound like the profile of a calculating killer to me. He doesn't sound like he's up to the job of murdering anyone."

But anxiety was making Annabelle belligerent. She lifted her chin. "Explain this, then: Why—if this Neil is so devoted to religion—have I never seen him? I'm the vicar at the only church in this village, yet I have never come across him."

"Perhaps he has been to your services. They've been rather packed lately. You might have missed him."

"Impossible," Annabelle answered instantly. "The congregation has to pass me on the way out. Are you suggesting he sneaks out the back to avoid me? I know every person at my services. When I'm in the pulpit, if I see a face I don't know, I keep it in mind so I can speak to them later. I've seen no one like this Neil."

"Well, maybe he's of a different denomination then." Annabelle opened her mouth but, finding she had no retort this time, she closed it without saying anything. "Really, Annabelle, this Neil character being the murderer seems a bit of a stretch to me."

"Hmm, well, I think this is a"—Annabelle waved at the charred remains on the lawn—"a warning."

"Of what?"

"Of something."

"Listen," Mike said comfortingly. "I promise I'll do everything I can to find this Neil fellow. It shouldn't take long; he seems to have worked for every employer in the village. Once I do, I'll take him in and question him thoroughly. Until then, it's probably best if you just stay as safe as possible. No midnight jaunts across the moors chasing shadows, and definitely no trying to find this Neil for yourself. Think about the wedding—I'm sure there's plenty to do

—and leave this investigation to me. I'm throwing everything at it. It's got to be sorted by the wedding on Saturday, and there's a promotion to be won. I couldn't be more motivated."

Annabelle took a deep breath, unable to disagree with Mike when he used his firm but compassionate voice. And also, when he was being completely logical. "Okay," she said reluctantly. Mike almost believed her for a second.

"This is a bad omen," Philippa said when Annabelle got in her car. The elderly woman looked over at the sorry pile of cinders as she wrung her hands. Her eyes had lit up when she heard Mike encouraging Annabelle to focus on the wedding arrangements, but now they were ablaze with fury and determination. "But there's no way I'm letting anyone ruin this wedding, demonic witch-hunter or not!"

CHAPTER TWENTY-FIVE

FAMISHED BUT FACING another long day, Mike agreed to drop by the church cottage to pick up some food at Annabelle's insistence. He followed her blue Mini Cooper and parked in the churchyard in a manner Annabelle found only merely acceptable.

"There wasn't anything left over after our dinner last night, it was so delicious," Annabelle said as they waited for Philippa to unlock the door. "But I kept some back before we started, enough for you to have for lunch."

"Fantastic!" Mike said as they followed Philippa into the cottage. "I would have probably forgotten to eat today entirely. I've got so much to do."

"That's why a man like you needs a wife," Philippa announced ahead of them as she made her way into the kitchen. She immediately put the kettle on. "You men would let yourself go to ruin if it weren't for us women. Did you know that married men live longer than unmarried ones?"

"And why is that, Philippa?" Mike asked her mildly. After a shaky start, he was beginning to get the hang of her.

"Because we nag you to go to the doctor."

"Not to death then."

"Humph." Philippa scowled, but she was getting the hang of him too. A little twinkle appeared in her eye, and she gently swatted him with her tea towel.

Annabelle rolled her eyes at their exchange as she went to prepare Mike's plate of food. Whilst he waited, Mike relaxed. He'd had an early start, even earlier than the call to attend the site of the burned marquee, and as much as he liked to think of himself as a modern man, he couldn't deny the satisfaction of having something delicious and soul-enriching prepared for him.

"Will you have a cup of tea?" Philippa asked.

"No, thanks," Mike replied. "I'll just take the food and go if that's alright."

"Oh, go on!" Philippa urged. "You can spare five minutes!"

"I'm sorry, no. I know it appears rude, but it's the job. The hours immediately after a murder is committed are the most crucial. We're already twenty-four hours in."

"What about your stag do? If there's no time for a cup of tea, what about that?"

"Stag do? If this murderer isn't caught soon, I can't have a stag do. What would it look like to the villagers? To my men? No parties for me when other people are sacrificing and working hard. No indeed."

"What are you going to do next?" Annabelle asked.

Mike sighed heavily. "I've put a call out telling the team to prioritise looking for this Neil character, but I'd like to do some digging myself. I'll visit Katie Flynn at the tearoom and Barbara at the Dog and Duck and ask them about him. At the very least, I should be able to get a better description of him for my officers."

Annabelle popped a lid onto a tub containing beef Wellington, peas, roast potatoes, and gravy from the evening before. She ladled plum charlotte into another container, topping the dessert with Cornish ice cream that would melt into the crunchy fruit topping, making it moist and creamy. Placing the food into a carrier bag along with utensils and a napkin, she said, "How did your visit to the travellers go?"

Mike took the bag from her. "Thanks. It went about as well as you warned me it would. For all our talk of witches, I spoke to a woman there who would appear to be quite the closest I've ever come to one. She called herself Jonquil—that's French for daffodil. She was old and wizened and missing half her teeth. Can't say I've ever seen anyone look less like a daffodil, but she did look like the witch she said she was."

"You didn't really go the travellers' camp, did you?" Philippa said, astonished. "What on earth could you want with those awful people? Are they the ones behind all of this?"

"Philippa!" Annabelle chided. "How judgemental of you!"

"Have you not heard the stories?"

Annabelle folded her arms, glaring. "I'm sure they're very entertaining and completely slanderous!"

"There's no smoke without fire," Philippa said, taking the kettle off the stove just as it was about to whistle.

CHAPTER TWENTY-SIX

"WHAT STORIES?" MIKE asked.

"Don't encourage her, Mike, please."

"I'm sorry, Annabelle, but I can't afford to dismiss things before hearing them at least—not at this point."

"Well," Philippa said, as she spooned tea into the pot, "apparently half of them aren't even real travellers, but murderers and criminals that are pretending to be gypsies so they can escape detection. They join these groups and simply carry on committing their crimes, evading capture as they travel around!" Annabelle folded her arms and looked up at the ceiling.

"You'd do worse than looking at them if you want to solve your murder, Inspector," Philippa continued. "I've heard that they intend to take over the whole village. That they think this land is hallowed ground or something, and that it belongs to them. They want to reclaim it, and they don't care who they have to harm in order to do it!"

"Philippa, you're better than this," Annabelle said, despite knowing perfectly well that her church secretary wasn't. "These fear-mongering tales and ridiculous notions have a basis in nothing but ignorance, overactive imaginations, and gossip."

Mike chuckled lightly. "I'd have to agree with Annabelle on that," he said. "I've been to their camp, and most of their community appears to consist of women and children."

"Do you think they would parade their beasts for a police officer? Of course not! They saw you coming and hid away. I'm sure of it," Philippa said as if it were the most obvious thing in the world.

Mike paused for a moment. Philippa's idea of marauding travellers avenging some ancient theft of lands was difficult to believe, but still unsettling.

"When you visited them," Philippa continued as she picked cups from the cabinets and placed them on the counter, "did you ask them what they're doing here?"

"They're travellers, Philippa," said Annabelle.

"Well, they don't seem to like moving very much considering all the fuss they made when they were asked to shift from the Websters' property!"

Mike blew out his cheeks. He held his palm up when Annabelle opened her mouth to argue with Philippa some more. "The Websters' property?" he asked. "Where Kathleen Webster was killed?" Mike thought back to seeing the man-bear at the farm and later at the travellers' camp.

At his sharp tone, Philippa looked up from the tiny bowl into which she was precariously tipping sugar from a huge bag. The bag was almost as big as Philippa, and Annabelle looked on doubtfully as she thought back to her school physics lessons. A sugary, powdery avalanche seemed likely.

"Yes," Philippa said. "The Websters' land extends a

long way, much further than you'd expect. They neglect most of it. Theirs was the first place those gypsies settled—in the woods just north of the smallholding."

"Are the Webster sisters the ones who made them move?" Mike asked.

"Not exactly. The tensions came from a variety of sources. Locals hunt in woods bordering the Websters' property, and that's where all the arguments and bad feelings started."

Annabelle noticed Mike brooding. "Please be careful if you're thinking of visiting them again," she said. "There's been enough antagonism between the village and the travellers already. It's only just settled down, but it could so easily flare up again."

"Hmph! Given that you think them harmless, you certainly sound like you know as well as I do how dangerous they are," Philippa said. Annabelle gave her a black look. Philippa was getting on her last nerve.

"It's not that they are dangerous as such, Philippa," Annabelle argued. "Just that relations with the village are tense and potentially combustible. Even the gentlest of people get riled up with enough provocation."

"Don't worry," Mike said in a tone cheerier than he felt. "I'm not planning on breaking down any doors just yet. There are already plenty of threads to pull on. No need to provoke anyone right at this moment." He pushed himself out of his chair. "Okay, I'm off. Thank you, Philippa, for the information. And thank you, my darling, for the food and the love."

He smiled, kissed Annabelle quickly, and headed for the door. Annabelle watched him for three seconds, cast a quick glance at Philippa, and hurried after him. "Wait! I'm coming with you!"

"Hmm?" Mike grunted as he stopped in the open doorway.

"I'm coming with you," Annabelle said firmly. "If you're looking for someone, then there's no better guide to the village than me. Besides, you said yourself that I should stay safe, and I can't think of a safer place, or one where I'd rather be, than alongside you."

"Annabelle!" Philippa exclaimed. "You promised me that we'd prepare the children's activities for the reception! And the wedding favours! And go over the schedule for the speeches!"

Mike looked from one woman to another, wishing he could vanish. At the very least he wanted to stymie the argument that he was about to be party to.

"I'm sorry, Philippa," Annabelle said, pulling on her coat. "This is far too important for me not to help the inspector. Especially when I could be in danger myself."

"The only danger you're in is that of having the most shambolic wedding imaginable!" Philippa cried.

"I'm sorry," Annabelle repeated as she grabbed Mike's arm, dragging him behind her out of the cottage. "I'll try to get back as soon as I can."

The door banged shut. Philippa stared at it before looking up at the ceiling and muttering in a low, helpless voice, "Just one sign, Lord. One sign, and I'll happily shake that woman until she comes to her senses!"

CHAPTER TWENTY-SEVEN

ANNABELLE PREPARED HERSELF for another wincing, armrest-clenching, footwell-pressing ride as the passenger in Mike's car. At least today was nicer than yesterday. The clouds had departed, leaving the sky a clear, bright blue. The air was fresh.

"We found out some rather interesting things about the book we discovered at Kathleen Webster's," Annabelle said as Mike performed a four-point turn to get out of the churchyard. Three would have sufficed in Annabelle's opinion.

"What book?" he asked.

"The book we found under Kathleen Webster's mattress."

"Really? You didn't mention it earlier."

"It's the journal of a young woman pursued by a witch-hunter."

Mike slammed on the brakes. Annabelle pitched forwards before falling back against her seat. "What!

Where? Who is this woman? We should talk to her right now!"

"No, silly," Annabelle said, adjusting her seatbelt after the jolt and brushing her hair out of her face. "The book was written in the 1800s."

Disappointment spread across the inspector's features. "What relevance could it possibly have now then?" he asked, the letdown leaving him churlish. He took his foot off the brake and let the car roll into the lane. "That our victim enjoyed reading fairy tales about witches?"

"Perhaps it's more than that," Annabelle said. "What connection did Kathleen have to Martha George? That's the name of the woman who wrote the journal. What could Kathleen want with a book like that? She'd had it since she was a teenager. Joan said she found it under the floorboards. Did she have a particular interest in witches? Or perhaps Kathleen was a witch—I mean, thought she was—and that was what convinced the murderer to kill her. And what has happened to her cat?"

Mike sighed as he drove the car along the street which led to Katie Flynn's tea shop. "Perhaps," he said, shrugging.

Annabelle frowned at Mike's lack of interest, studying his face for a sign of what was wrong. "Is everything alright?" she asked.

"What?" Mike said, turning to her and seeing how concerned she looked. "Yes. Of course. It's just this case. I can't tell what's relevant and what isn't anymore. Witches, books, travellers, this Neil chap. And time's moving on. I need a breakthrough."

"It'll become clear, don't worry." Annabelle smiled. "We just need to winkle a bit more."

Mike parked the car outside the tea shop. He turned off the engine but remained deflated.

"Plus..." he murmured reluctantly.

"Yes?" Annabelle sat up in her seat, suddenly alert.

"I've been thinking and . . . I wanted to ask you something..."

"Yes?"

"Actually, never mind. Let's go."

"Wait!" Annabelle said, grabbing his arm as he reached for the car door. "Ask me, go on."

"It's nothing." Mike smiled meekly. "Just a stupid thought. We should get this done so I can go back to the station."

"Don't be silly!" Annabelle chuckled. "You can ask me anything! We can't begin having secrets before we're even married."

Mike shut the door again and took a deep breath. "Well . . . How should I put this? When you talk about this investigation, you talk about it with such curiosity and concern. I understand why—it's one of the many reasons I adore you. You genuinely care when there is injustice and want to do your utmost to set things right and find the truth..."

Annabelle smiled. "Yes."

"But we're getting married in just a few days," Mike continued, "and we rarely even talk about it. Philippa told me that you've been reluctant to finish many of the preparations, and I'm getting the impression you're avoiding something—something to do with our wedding."

He regarded Annabelle carefully. "This wedding is supposed to be one of the most special days of our lives and . .. well... it sometimes seems like you're a little unenthusiastic about it, that's all."

Mike looked at Annabelle, nervously anticipating her response. He omitted telling her about Jonquil's premonition. It had kept him up the night before, an ominous reminder of the sleepless nights he'd had as he tried to summon the courage to propose. The picture Jonquil had painted of Annabelle jilting him at the altar was still as vivid in his mind as it had been the day before.

"I see . . ." Annabelle said slowly. Her face was blank as she considered his words.

"You're not . . . you're not . . ." Mike took a deep breath. "Having second thoughts about marrying me, are you?" he asked tentatively.

"Of course not!" Annabelle said emphatically. She coughed. "Are you?"

"Absolutely not!" Mike exclaimed. "I'm fine!"

"As I, too, am fine."

"So, everything's fine."

"Everything is fine."

"Fine."

"Fine."

They looked at each other with forced smiles. An awkward silence that each was desperate for the other to fill grew between them.

"Let's talk to Katie Flynn then," Mike said finally.

"Yes," Annabelle said. "Let's."

CHAPTER TWENTY-EIGHT

"HALLOOOOOO!" WHEN ANNABELLE and Mike entered, Katie Flynn, owner of Flynn's tearoom, couldn't abandon her position behind the counter fast enough. "How are you two lovebirds? Ready for your big day?"

Oblivious to the awkward conversation Annabelle and Mike had just had, Katie showered the couple with questions about the wedding. She was joined by her customers, who all decided that now was the perfect occasion upon which to interrogate the couple.

"Have you chosen the flowers?"

"Where's the honeymoon then?"

"Could my Fluffy be the ring bearer?"

"Sit down, sit down. I'm all ready for you," Katie said. Katie was providing desserts for the wedding reception. She had been waiting anxiously for Annabelle's visit, and with time now short, she was determined to trap them in her tearoom and hold them hostage to cake. Their ransom? Decisions about which desserts they wanted for their reception.

"What can I tempt you with?" Katie said. "Scones and clotted cream, cake, chocolate mousse, fondant fancies, hot chocolate bombs?" Cakes and sweets of all kinds were quickly laid out in front of Annabelle and Mike. "Now, you try each one and tell me what you think. And I've got custard tarts in the oven. If you wait long enough for them to cool, you can try them too. The customers love them. They're always gone in a couple of hours. There's a queue outside at opening time on the days I bake them."

The problem for Mike was that the tasting—along with the other ladies of the village who told stories of how long they had waited for their vicar to find a lifelong companion and how delighted they were that she finally had, and who then proceeded to instruct Annabelle in exactly what she needed to do in order to retain a man as fine as the inspector—left barely any opportunity for him to ask the questions of Katie that he intended.

"So lovely to see you have a young man, Vicar—finally."

"We were beginning to think it would never happen, didn't we, Maureen?"

"You took your time alright. But you made it."

"A slick of red lippy when you hear his car in the driveway; that's my advice."

Forty minutes and seventeen cakes later, Annabelle had forgotten about the investigation and was asking herself why she hadn't got around to this part of the wedding preparations earlier. As she slipped into a sugar coma, the inspector managed to ask Katie about the mysterious man she had hired a few days ago.

"Katie, I heard that you employed someone to run some deliveries for you. Can you tell me anything about him?"

Katie wiped her palms on her apron and pulled a face. "Nothing but that he was literally good for nothing. Thank goodness my reputation is solid and he did nothing to damage it. Absolutely useless he was. I like to give everyone a chance but some people..."

"What can you tell me about where he came from? What happened to him?"

"He turned up on my doorstep like a stray cat one morning, looking for work. He seemed nice enough, but short of being presentable and having a van, I can't say much about him. He wasn't a local, I know that. But I don't know where he is now. I'm sorry, that's all I can tell you. He was gone in a day."

"Alright, thanks."

"Have you made a decision?"

"Hmm?"

Katie nodded at the plates on the table, all of which now contained merely the crumbs of her entire cake display. They both looked at Annabelle, who was still munching slowly, her eyes half-closed with sugar-induced delirium.

"I think we're way beyond making decisions, Katie," Mike said. "Sorry. I'll take her home to sleep it off and have her get back to you."

As Mike escorted a droopy Annabelle from the tea shop, Katie called from the doorway to remind them to come back soon. He walked to the car feeling like they had wasted their time despite the piles of boxes filled with treats that they left with.

At the Dog and Duck, the environment provided a far lower level of distraction. It was too early for the pub to be busy, and the regulars, all male, focused on their pints with barely a glance at the newcomers. Landlady Barbara was in fine fettle, though. "Good morning, my lovelies! Can I get—"

"No," Mike interrupted her quickly, eager to avoid a

repeat experience of the one they'd had at Flynn's. Sampling the drinks for the wedding would have rendered him useless, and he was keen not to end up like Annabelle, who was now almost asleep. Mike sat Annabelle in a corner. She murmured quietly, and satisfied she'd come to no harm, he walked to the bar to ask Barbara a few incisive questions about Neil.

"I don't know, luvvie. I just chased him out the door after the third mistake. He was here one minute, gone the next. That's all I can tell you."

Defeated, Mike pushed away from the bar. Annabelle was snoring quietly in the corner where he had left her. "Inspector!" A stout, manly arm wrapped itself around Mike's shoulders. Mike jumped. "May we call you Mike?"

CHAPTER TWENTY-NINE

"YOU'RE PRACTICALLY ONE of our village family! And very soon you will be." It was Dr. Whitefield, the vet. Mike had only seen him from afar, but now up close, he could see what Annabelle meant when she said he looked like a cow.

"Er, thanks. Actually, can you tell me anything about the Webster sisters? Did you ever go there to see to their animals?"

"I did, as a matter of fact. Not often, but I was up there recently. They had a goat that was lame."

"Did you notice anything awry?"

"Not really. Thought the place could use a bit of care and attention. I spoke to Kathleen about yard hygiene. Not sure she took it in. She was mostly concerned about her goat; she always did look upon her animals as pets, which never bodes well in a farmer, I find. No, everything seemed normal. Nothing much wrong with the goat."

"You didn't see anyone hanging about?"

Dr. Whitefield thought back. "No, no. I didn't see

anyone at all. I'm sorry I can't help you. Now, can I buy you a drink?" He slapped Mike on the shoulder.

Now that someone had taken the lead, the regulars moved in. For the next fifteen minutes, Mike was instructed in the secrets of pleasing a wife by a number of self-appointed, beer-soaked experts.

"Don't forget to put down the toilet seat and the lid."

"Always have a place to get away to and don't tell her where it is."

"The bins. Always take out the bins."

With apologies and explanations about the demands of a murder investigation, Mike extracted himself from the attentions of his persecutors, picked up a dozy Annabelle by the arm, and hastily left the pub as a chorus of "Just one more!" and "See you soon!" chased them out the door.

"It's like we're celebrities. I've never had so many free things thrown my way," Mike said.

"I could get used to that part," Annabelle mumbled.

"Or nuggets of unasked-for advice."

"I'm not so keen on that part."

"What do they take us for?"

"They are showing their love for us."

"Is that what you call it?"

Annabelle laughed, refreshed after her nap. She linked her arm in Mike's as they walked to the car.

"Hello, Annabelle!"

"Father John! How are you this fine morning?"

Father John patted his rounded stomach. "I'm very well, thank you, especially after that wonderful meal last night. Morning, Mike." Mike nodded a greeting.

"Where are you off to?" Annabelle asked her former mentor.

"Just going to meet Samuel Bellingham again for a

quick drink. How are things? Are you making progress with the investigation?"

Annabelle and Mike shrugged at the same time. "It's a slow one," Mike answered.

"How about the book?" Annabelle asked. "Any progress there?

"Actually, the book is fascinating," Father John said, his eyes lighting up. "I've made my way through almost the entire thing, and I've been writing up some of the more interesting passages. Apparently, this Edward Butterworth fellow—"

"The follower of Matthew Hopkins, the original witch-hunter?" Annabelle asked, ignoring Mike's almost inaudible groan.

"Yes. Apparently, his whole family were followers of this Matthew Hopkins chap, even two centuries later. Took it upon themselves to continue his work and hunt down women they supposed were witches, even in the 1800s. This would appear to include Martha, the owner of the journal. Frightful family."

"I see . . ." Annabelle said.

"I did a little more searching online, and—it was the oddest thing—it seems like the entire Butterworth family were male. There are absolutely no reports of girls being born to them."

"Perhaps it was a genetic trait," Mike said coolly. He was alert to a stop in the conversation through which he could make his escape. He had much to do.

"More like they wanted it that way," Annabelle said, scowling at the thought. "They probably made sure of it."

"Indeed," Father John said. "Anyway, with what I know now, I thought it would be good to show the journal to Bellingham and get his historical perspective on things. Not sure it has any bearing on your case, Mike, but it's jolly interesting."

"Tell us if you find anything," Annabelle said. "Not sure how it might be pertinent, but you never know."

"Will do."

Father John walked on, and Annabelle and Mike returned to the inspector's car. It was midday now, the sky still a clear blue, no sign of any clouds or rain. Annabelle wondered if the good weather would hold for their wedding.

"The post-mortem results should be in soon," Mike said, looking at his watch. "I need to get back to the station."

"I'll come with you," Annabelle said.

"Are you sure? Philippa is probably waiting for you."

Annabelle squirmed in her seat, her eyes fixed forwards.

"I'd like to hear Harper's report. I couldn't sit around filling goody bags and studying seating plans with so much on my mind anyway. There's plenty of time for all that."

Her words caused a pulse of fear to ripple through Mike's body. Jonquil's prophecy flashed through his mind. With each rendition, it only became more vivid. He started the car, and they drove off.

CHAPTER THIRTY

ANNABELLE FOLLOWED MIKE as he strode into the village police station. It was often clear what mood Mike was in by the way he walked. A swaggering saunter when he felt at ease; a tense, hunched-over trudge when he had things on his mind; and a striding, powerful march when he knew exactly what he wanted—like now, for instance.

"Raven!" he barked without breaking step. "How close are we to finding this Neil person I called you about?"

PC Raven wiped his brow. "Nowhere near, sir. I've checked every record available to me and nothing comes up."

"He could live in a nearby town, perhaps even as far as Truro, although that's rather a long way," Annabelle suggested.

"It's not that far, Annabelle. It just seems like it. A completely different environment," Mike said.

"Yes," Annabelle replied. "Quite."

"I thought of that," Raven explained. "Found a few Neils around, questioned them, and well, to cut a long story short, none of them are the man you're looking for. Derbyshire's out asking around, but he hasn't turned up anything. A photo or a last name would help, sir."

"We don't have either. Keep looking. Focus on the local area. Can't be that hard to find him, not in a small place like this," Mike instructed, ignoring the fact that his own efforts had been failures.

"Perhaps he's moved on," Annabelle said.

"Let's hope not. He could be anywhere if that's the case."

"Didn't Gabriella say he was from a 'den of sin'?"

Mike thought for a second, then nodded. "Yes. You think that's real?"

"I don't know." Annabelle shrugged. "But it might be a clue. Where around here could be considered a 'den of sin'?"

"The post-mortem results are in. I left them on your desk, sir," Raven called out as the inspector walked through to the back office.

Mike nodded approvingly and picked up the blue file. He began to thumb his way through the report.

"Anything, um, noteworthy?" Annabelle asked.

"She died of blunt force trauma to the back of the head. No suggestion of weapon, though. The pitchfork was mostly cosmetic, as Harper predicted."

"So, she wasn't actually killed by the pitchfork?" Annabelle said.

"No," Mike said. "Why?"

"It fits with the idea that the pitchfork was put there afterwards to trap her soul. You know, like that Bellingham fellow said. That someone thought she was a witch."

"It could also be that someone was trying to make it look

like a witch killing," Mike said, still thumbing through the file. "To distract us, send us in the wrong direction."

There was a knock at the door, and Harper appeared, looking a little pale. "Inspector, there you are. How are things?" She nodded at the file in Mike's hand. "What did you think of the post-mortem results?"

"You didn't do it yourself, did you?" Annabelle asked, appalled at the idea that Harper, her professionalism notwithstanding, would perform a post-mortem on her own aunt.

"No, I got a colleague to do it. I just came to see if you'd made any progress. How's it going?"

"There's so little information, we could come up with theories all day," Mike said. "There's no suggestion of a murder weapon. Are we sure she was murdered?"

"What do you mean?" Annabelle asked.

"Well, could she have slipped? Hit her head on the cobbles? An accident. It was greasy in that farmyard. Dr. Whitefield said he talked to Kathleen about it. He called it 'yard hygiene.'"

"But what about the pitchfork? Funny kind of accident, that."

Mike conceded the point. "Doesn't look good, I agree. But technically, the pitchfork didn't cause her death. Maybe an opportunist came along afterwards."

"A witch hunting one just happened by? Just like that?"

Mike put his hands up. "Okay, okay. It was just an idea." He clapped the file shut and looked at Harper sternly. "Listen, Harper, I know you're professional enough to understand why I might ask this, but it's a bit awkward."

Harper rocked on her heels. "I know what you're going to say," she said. Mike tilted his head as he waited for her to read his mind. "You're going to ask me if I think her sister, Joan, could be a suspect."

Mike broke into a wry smile. "Yes." Harper thought like a good detective.

"Rationally," she said, sighing deeply, "I know you're right to wonder that. It's obvious she's not of completely sound mind, and of course, if she's capable of saying such nonsensical things, it's only logical to assume she might be capable of actually doing something equally irrational."

Annabelle placed a comforting hand on the woman's shoulder. "Has she been getting worse?" she asked.

"It's difficult to say. Aunt Joan's always been a little loopy, highly strung."

"When you asked her about the book we found, she said that she'd come to your family when she was fourteen. What did she mean by that?"

"Oh, Joan's adopted."

Annabelle bit her lip for a second. "Joan's adopted?" she asked. "But you look so much like her!"

"Yes," Harper said before laughing gently. "It's a common misconception. Everyone in my family always jokes about it. I look more like Aunt Joan than I do my own mother, despite sharing no DNA with her at all. Just a strange coincidence. My father—Kathleen's brother— told me Joan always had a bit of a complex about being adopted. Her early life before she came to them was very difficult. We always thought that must account for her strangeness." She turned to Mike. "But the sisters were very close. Kathleen inherited the smallholding from my grandfather, but when Joan's husband died, there was no question that Joan would move in and help her with it."

"And who stands to gain from Kathleen's death?"

"I do," Harper said bluntly. "Kathleen never married.

No children. My father has passed, so I own the farm now." Harper shrugged.

"But what will happen to Joan?" Annabelle asked.

"It's in the will that Joan can stay in the house for as long as she needs. This was all agreed years ago. Joan knows about it, but whether she remembers is a different matter. On the surface, everything remains the same. I'll have to do something about running the farm though. As for the idea that Joan would kill her sister, it doesn't make sense. They rubbed along well enough, helped one another out. They could be crotchety with one another, but they weren't violent, let alone capable of attacking each other with pitchforks. Besides, she says she went to Truro."

"We do have CCTV footage of her getting off the bus at the bus depot at seven p.m.," Mike admitted.

"The last bus to Truro leaves at five thirty p.m., and the first one arrives here at nine a.m. Kathleen was killed sometime between six p.m. and six a.m., so Joan couldn't have done it. My honest answer, Inspector, as best as I can offer, is no, I don't think Joan murdered Kathleen."

"Okay. Thanks, Harper," Mike said. "I'll exhaust my other options before I come back to the idea again."

Raven appeared at his doorway. "Inspector, call for you from Truro. They want to go over a few details relating to the case."

"Put it through."

Harper looked at Annabelle and said, "Would you like some tea?"

Annabelle thought of Philippa. A pang of guilt ran through her. "Yes, I'd love some," she replied.

CHAPTER THIRTY-ONE

ANNABELLE FOLLOWED HARPER to the corner of the main office where the tea making supplies were kept. The pathologist pulled out a desk chair for Annabelle and turned on the electric kettle. Annabelle allowed herself to relax as she watched Harper make the tea, enjoying the lithe, graceful movements of the elegant woman without the restless feelings of mild jealousy she used to feel towards her.

"Sugar?" Harper asked.

"Two, please. I'm on a diet."

Harper smiled as she dropped two cubes of sugar into a mug and stirred. She placed it on the desk next to Annabelle and took a seat.

"I did some research into Martha George. It's not hard these days with the internet. It seems that she and I are related! She's my great-great-great grandmother."

Annabelle's eyes widened. "Really?"

"Around the time she wrote that journal, it seems Martha married Conor Webster, a local farmer. They had a child. And lived happily, it seemed. She came from London originally, a long way in those days. Anyhow, she never got caught by the witch-hunters. She must have felt safe down here, settled, and lived out her life as a farmer's wife."

"I wonder how she married a second time given that she was already married to someone who gave her up as a witch?"

"Oh, he died. I looked him up too."

"Did you find anything about the baby she fled with?"

"No, there was nothing. Just the mention of a new baby, a girl."

Annabelle's eyes narrowed. "Hmm, I wonder."

"What do you mean?"

"Perhaps there was no new baby. Perhaps Conor Webster agreed to accept the baby as his own to save Martha's reputation or even her skin."

"You mean, it was all a cover-up to push the witch-hunters off the scent?"

"Yes. I wonder if she hid her baby and confided in a good, decent man who covered for them."

"To save them from being found by the people chasing her?"

"Uh-huh. Martha and Conor might have lived a quiet life on the farm and concocted a story around the baby's birth."

Harper pursed her lips as she thought about this. "Was that really necessary? I mean, as a widow, she didn't have to worry about being seen as an unwed mother."

"No, but it would have circumvented gossip and suspicion if someone came looking for a lone woman stranger travelling with a baby of a certain age. Remember, a hundred and seventy years ago it was a lot easier to fudge this kind of thing, especially out here in the countryside. In the circumstances, it would have been a great outcome for her." Annabelle sat back in her chair. "Yes, I like that story. Perhaps Martha hid her past and put the notebook under the floorboards so no one could find it."

"But many years later, Kathleen did."

Annabelle nodded. "Yes, perhaps she did."

"How fascinating!"

The two women sipped their tea in silence as they digested the story. Harper broke the silence. "You have my sympathy, Annabelle."

"Sympathy?"

"Well, you have so much going on—your parish, this case. And just as you're about to get married. It must feel overwhelming."

"I suppose," Annabelle said. She focused on her tea, blowing on it so hard the surface rippled and spat a drop of tea back at her, stinging her on the nose.

"I imagine it's caused all sorts of problems with your planning and nerves. All this business of murder and witches and burning marquees can't help you prepare for a lovely day."

"Oh, you heard about the marquee?"

"Hard not to in a village this small and excited. Mrs. Sutton at my B and B can't stop talking about it. Must be very difficult. So much attention."

"In a sense," Annabelle said, now trying not to scald her tongue as she sipped.

"If you need any help, you know you can count on me. I'm just biding time here, doing odd bits of work and dealing with Aunt Kathleen's things. Also assessing what to do about Aunt Joan, of course. She can't deal with the farm alone."

"Thank you. Are you looking forward to your husband arriving?"

Harper smiled. "I am. It'll be good to see him."

"He'll help you with the cows!"

"Yes, he'll get stuck right in. It's good to know he has my back and I'm not alone." Harper smiled. There was a pause. "I remember when I got married," Harper said, her eyes misty. "I was a nervous wreck."

"Really?" Annabelle said, suddenly attentive. "I can't imagine you being nervous over anything."

Harper chuckled easily. "Oh yes! I was about the same age as you are now, and very independent. I loved my career and was focused so very hard on it. I'd travelled, seen the world, lived in big cities, very much the girl-about-town. I felt like marriage and coming down here to live in this part of the world would be the end of my life as I knew it. Which it was, of course, but I was quite unsure about that part of it. I'd said yes because I loved Nick so much. But I had very mixed feelings about it."

Annabelle gazed at her, astonished. "Did you? Gosh, I never would have thought."

"Well, there you go." Harper smiled, taking another slow sip. "I must admit, you're taking all this chaos incredibly well. Better than I would have in the circumstances."

Annabelle looked down at her tea as she allowed nagging concerns and dark worries that she'd been tucking away to bubble up to the surface.

"Actually," Annabelle said, slowly, "I'm rather anxious myself."

Harper tilted her head, put her cup down, and leant forwards. "Really?"

"Yes." Annabelle felt tears gathering, her eyes aching with the pressure. She looked down again. A huge swell of emotion stirred in her, her anxieties threatening to burst forth.

Harper scooted nearer on her chair and put a hand on the reverend's knee. "Tell me, Annabelle," Harper urged.

Annabelle looked up and smiled when she saw the genuine friendship in the pathologist's eyes. "I don't even know how to articulate it really. It's just that . . . Well . . . I've never been the most girlish of women, you know. When I was a child, I was always the tomboy, climbing trees and scraping my knees. My brother called me Bumble. I thought it was because I was always busy, but I found out later it was because I bumbled around, clumsy. I never sat around combing my doll's hair or wondering if a prince would come and sweep me away to his castle. I'd have pretended to be a pirate or an adventurer over a princess."

Harper laughed, and Annabelle smiled at her own silliness. "You're still very much an adventurer, Annabelle," Harper said.

"And that's the problem. Everyone seems to be so excited about this wedding, and so intent on placing me in the centre, the role of the beautiful bride—yet I simply feel unfit for it. Unworthy, even."

"Oh, Annabelle! That's nonsense!"

"Is it? I don't think I've had a normal conversation for months! All anyone wants to talk about is my dress, or the ceremony, or my vows. I feel more like a prize marrow being prepared for the summer fête than a woman about to commit to spending the rest of her life with the man she loves! I feel this wedding is for the benefit of everyone else rather than the two people that matter. And I feel the weight of expectation. I'm a little resentful, if I'm honest. I've prayed and prayed for resolution, but there's been no answer. And we're just two days away!"

Harper smiled and squeezed Annabelle's knee. "Everyone loves you. They want to make you happy, and that makes them happy. You're in a special position. When there's such a lot of joy and love, things take on a life of their own. But your feelings can get a little lost amongst all the energy. It's important to remember the main thing: that it's just one day. The most important thing is that you and Mike get married and then have decades of health and happiness together." Harper patted Annabelle on her knee and leant back. "The wedding will be over before you know it," she said reassuringly. "To be perfectly honest, I don't even remember mine. One minute I was nervously being taken to the church, and the next I was enjoying cocktails with my husband on a cruise ship. Without the photos, I would have doubted that it even happened!"

Harper stopped herself and sighed gently. "Look at me being silly, lecturing a vicar of all people on marriage!"

"No, it's not silly at all," Annabelle insisted. "I think that's exactly what I needed to hear, honestly. With all the talk of elaborate decorations, seating plans, and once-in-a-lifetime moments, things that are not my forte, I think I've lost sight of what it's all about, and I've started fussing and worrying."

"What does your God say?"

"I don't know. I can't hear him above all the noise Philippa keeps making!" The two women laughed.

Harper smiled and sipped again from her teacup, looking up as the inspector emerged from his office. "Talk to Mike," she said quietly so he wouldn't hear. "I guarantee all your worries will disappear if you just talk to him."

"I will," Annabelle said, her previously pale cheeks now flushed.

"Annabelle, you're still here," Mike said. "Would you like a lift home?"

Annabelle looked at Harper, then turned back to the

inspector. "No, it's alright. I'll walk. The fresh air will do me good. Call me later, yes?"

"Will do." Mike, slightly relieved, went back into his office.

"Thanks, Harper. I appreciate your counsel."

"No problem, Annabelle. Have a good walk home."

As Annabelle picked up her bag, she thought about what Harper had said. There was something about her words that comforted her. But she still felt burdened with the truth—the whole truth that she still hadn't been able to say out loud.

CHAPTER THIRTY-TWO

BOOM! THE STATION doors burst open. Father John ran through them, his face wretched with distress. "Harper!" he called as soon as he noticed her. "Inspector! I'm glad I found you. Annabelle! Thank goodness you're all here."

"What is it?" Mike asked, coming out of his office.

Father John panted a few times as he caught his breath. "The book . . . It's gone . . ."

"What do you mean, gone?" Harper said.

"Martha George's journal?" Annabelle asked.

Father John nodded, breathing quickly as he gathered enough energy to explain. "I brought the book to the pub to discuss it with Bellingham. He took a look and had some very interesting things to say. Then . . . it was gone."

"It just disappeared?" Mike asked.

"Yes," Father John said. "We were in a booth by the door. The book was on the table, open, and then . . . There one minute, gone the next. We looked everywhere for it. Under the tables, in our bags. Nowhere."

"Someone must have pinched it," Harper said.

Mike nodded. "Who was in the pub with you?" he asked.

Father John's expression changed. His bushy eyebrows, which seemed to be communicating in a language of their own, dropped. He rubbed his brow roughly as if struggling to say something.

"What is it?" Annabelle urged. "Do you suspect someone?"

"Now look, I don't want to cast aspersions on anyone. I'm just telling you this as a matter of fact."

"Get to it," Mike ordered, his previous reserve and deference to Father John leaving him. "I don't have time for finer feelings. I've got a case to close by Friday night."

Father John swallowed and looked down. "Some people, a group, came into the bar shortly after we began talking. They were rather rowdy, and at one point I thought they were going to get in a fight with the regulars. But Barbara, I think that was her name, calmed everyone down. They left . . . and that was when I noticed the book was gone."

"Who were they?"

"Well, like I said, I don't want to cast asp—"

Mike interrupted him. "Come on, man. Are you going to help or not?"

"A group of travellers." Immediately, Annabelle looked across at Mike. His eyes were hard, flinty. "I regret to say that some of the people in the pub accused them without evidence. Things could have turned ugly."

"How many were there?" Mike asked.

"Ten? Twelve? I really can't say. Felt like a swarm of angry cows, if I'm honest. It was a bit unexpected and frightening, especially in a lovely village like this."

"Were they close to your table?"

Father John looked at Annabelle, her face almost pleading for some other answer.

"Somewhat," he said almost apologetically. "They brushed past us on their way out."

"Right," Mike announced as he drew his coat tight around him. "Raven!" Raven popped up from beneath the desk where he was searching for a paperclip, but where in reality he had been hiding. "You're coming with me!"

"Wait! Mike!" Annabelle pleaded, stepping between the inspector and the door. "Don't jump to rash conclusions! If you antagonise them, it could cause a riot across the whole village!"

Mike's jaw clenched, his eyes no less hard. PC Raven walked up behind him. He put on his cap as he stood confidently behind his superior, although his hand shook as he did so. "I don't intend to antagonise anyone. My intention is to uncover the truth, and if I have to drag it out of them, then that's what I'll do," Mike said.

"She's right, Inspector," Harper said. She moved to stand beside Annabelle. "The travellers don't respect the police, so we should tread carefully with regards to them. We could end up with a bigger problem. Softly, softly, eh?"

Mike held up his palms to indicate he didn't want to hear anymore. "You don't think I know that? That doesn't make them immune to the law."

"But what basis for suspicion is there?" Harper said.

"Exactly!" Annabelle added. "The book could still show up. It might have been one of the regulars who stole it. Maybe it slipped behind a cushion. We should all go look." Annabelle immediately started for the door.

Mike put his hand out to stop her. He sighed impatiently. "Look, everyone is agreed that this investigation is going nowhere. We've got a dead woman, an arson, and now a theft. The only lead we have is a bumbling labourer whom we can't find. We're questioning people in tea shops and pubs. All whilst a giant camp of potential criminals exists right here on our doorstep."

Annabelle shook her head vigorously. "Mike, I think you're acting hastily. If you're intent on going to the travellers' camp again, this time with reinforcements"—Annabelle nodded at PC Raven, who paled at the idea that he might be anything of the kind—"you should only do so when we have firm, incriminating facts. And you certainly shouldn't do so in such a temper!"

Mike looked to his side to check that Raven was with him, then looked back at the two women blocking his path. There was something about the set of his jaw and the wildness in his eyes that struck Annabelle as more emotional than normal. Like some inner demon had become unshackled and was running the show. "Facts, eh? The first time I visited the travellers I could tell there was something deeply off about that place, and the people in it. Now we're looking for this Neil and he's nowhere to be found. Coincidence? Could Neil's 'den of sin' be the camp itself? Will I find this Neil there? It's about the only place we haven't tried. Raven, where was the first place these travellers set up shop?"

"The dark woods, sir."

"The where?"

"The dark woods. That's what the locals call it, sir. It's on the Webster sisters' property."

Mike nodded. "There we are! Are those enough facts for you, ladies?" he said with an air of finality. "They set up their camp on the Websters' property whilst harbouring a witch, remember? Then after they're moved on, the owner of the property is murdered and left as though a witch herself!"

"That's all circumstantial, supposition, and gossip, Mike!" Annabelle said.

"It's enough for me," the inspector said as he stepped forwards.

Desperately, Annabelle said, "Let us go instead! Me and Harper. They might offer us a more welcome reception. Be more open and forthcoming."

"Yes!" Harper agreed. "We'll go instead of you."

"What? Absolutely not!" Mike said. He attempted to go around them, but Annabelle and Harper moved as one. They neatly sidestepped and blocked him from leaving.

"Look," Harper explained, "we're not police officers, so they won't immediately feel threatened, but we know enough about this case to ask the right questions."

Mike stared from one woman to the other, too shocked by the idea of them going to the camp to offer a counter-argument. Then he thought of one. "Annabelle," he said. "You're going to be my wife in just a few days. I can't allow you to put yourself in danger!"

An indignant expression crossed Annabelle's face. The moment she put her hands on her hips, the inspector realised he had made a grave mistake, and he had something coming to him. And it wasn't a kiss . . .

"I beg your pardon!" Annabelle said boldly. "I may be about to become your wife, Inspector Michael James Nichols, but I am not some delicate, wilting petal. I'm capable of forming my own decisions regarding my safety. Now, I am going to the travellers' camp to treat them with respect and courtesy and find out everything I can from them. If you insist on coming along and creating a hostile, combative environment, that is your choice, but I'd prefer it if you didn't."

Mike glowered. He looked at PC Raven, who offered no help at all as he looked at a crack in the ceiling. Mike looked back at the women but said nothing.

"Come on, Harper," Annabelle said, linking arms with her.

"Right with you, Vicar," Harper replied. They left the men in stunned silence to hurry to Harper's car. "Girl power!" Annabelle hissed. She looked back at the station. "And, well, really!"

CHAPTER THIRTY-THREE

AS MIKE HAD done the day before, Annabelle and Harper drew up to the gate next to the field on the far side of which the travellers' homes were scattered. A heavy silence descended between the two women. Peering over the ploughed field that was ready for crop planting, they could see the caravans and wagons scattered on a grass verge at the edge of the woods.

"What do you think we should ask them?" Harper said as she opened the gate.

Annabelle sighed gently. "Honestly, I'm not sure. I'm just glad it's us showing up instead of an irate Mike. Perhaps we should start by simply opening up some communication between us. Show them we come in peace. Have a chat, find out how they're doing. There's been far too much distance between the travellers and villagers for too long now."

Harper nodded and held the gate, waiting for Annabelle to join her before they trudged across the field towards the camp. The sun had remained bright in a blue sky throughout the day, but a slight breeze had cooled the temperature down to coat weather. Outside the caravans, women hung washing whilst watching the babies and toddlers. The children played on their makeshift football pitch with a ball that had received the attention of a bicycle pump at some point since Mike had visited the camp. A few men tinkered with a truck. A few more sipped from cans as they sat back on plastic chairs and enjoyed the spring afternoon weather.

Like the previous day, it was the children who first noticed the visitors. Unlike the day before, however, when the tall, hunched figure of the man who was clearly a police officer kicked their ball back to them, the children were not startled by the two women. The black-haired female visitor with green eyes was compellingly striking and mysterious. Her tall, bouncing companion with the clerical collar who held up the skirts of her black cassock as she crossed the field was also exotic. They were too unusual and far too sincere for the children to feel afraid. They were strangers, for sure, but the children, trained from birth to intuit safe people and places, knew these were the good kind. Their curiosity was up, not their defences.

So instead of running back to the camp yelling warnings, the children stopped their play and moved aside, clearing a path for the women. They waited patiently for them to cross the imaginary boundaries of their pitch, and when they had done so, with a shriek and a boot of the ball, the children continued playing.

Annabelle and Harper were close now, close enough to notice the twitching of net curtains at the windows of the caravans and smell sausages frying on an improvised grill fashioned from a metal barrel. They saw a horse tethered to a caravan eating an apple from a girl's hand and the raked plot in a corner of the semicircle that bore the first, distinctive sprouts of carrots and onions, an optimistic sign that the travellers believed they would still be in place when it came time to harvest. An elderly woman darned an old jumper, reluctant to let go of skills that made her useful even though it would cost almost nothing to replace the item of clothing. A large man threw a baby into the air, catching the tot with meaty, tattooed arms, wide smiles on both of their faces.

Annabelle and Harper saw all this and suddenly felt ridiculous for having approached the camp with such trepidation. It was difficult to comprehend that this group of people were, indeed, the same group of people the inspector had warned so much about, and of which the entire village often talked in hushed, anxious, sometimes angry whispers.

As Annabelle and Harper relaxed, the travellers paid them attention. Unlike the children, the adults glared at the newcomers, unnerved and alarmed; some quickly got up from their deckchairs to retreat to caravans whilst others hurriedly appeared at doorways to see what the visitors wanted. The old lady stopped her darning, and sausages were taken off the grill. The only sounds came from the occasional thump of the children's ball and the tinny sound of a radio inside one of the caravans. A few of the men came over, exchanging glances and shrugs with each other as they formed a welcome party. The tattooed man stopped playing with his child, clutching her close as he moved with the others to greet Annabelle and Harper.

"What do you want?" the tattooed man asked.

Annabelle and Harper looked at each other before Annabelle answered. "My name is Reverend Annabelle. I live in the village. I'm the parish vicar. This is Harper Jones, our local . . . scientist. We'd just like to talk to some of you, if that's alright."

The men glanced at one another, considering her

request and looking for signs from each other as to whether to grant it. A woman's voice rose from one of the caravans. "Who is it?"

"Another preacher!" one of the men called back over his shoulder.

"Talk about what?" the tattooed man asked Annabelle. He thrust a big, stubble-covered cleft chin at her. It was so large, it reminded Annabelle of a long-abandoned bicycle stand she'd found in her shed when she moved into her cottage.

"Well . . ." Annabelle began tentatively. "I've been meaning to come and talk to you for quite a while now. I understand that relations with the people in the village haven't always been the best . . ."

"Pfft!" one of the men grunted. "The only relations they want are those where we're chased from our camp so that they can burn it to the ground." The other men murmured in agreement.

"I know," Annabelle said, bowing her head sympathetically. "And I agree that in many ways you've been treated unfairly. The gossip and rumours of the villagers have been rather unkind to you, and I hope to address those as much as I intend to assuage your opinion of the village."

"Ass—what?"

"Assuage. I mean, make things better," Annabelle replied. "Improve."

"Too late," the tattooed man with the prickly cleft chin said firmly, shaking his head. "You've done too much damage already. Treated us like scum from the second we arrived. It's too late for flowery words . . ." He looked Annabelle up and down, his earrings jangling, pausing at her ankles where the hem of her skirt was now trimmed with dirt. "And songs."

"Yeah," the male chorus around him hummed.

"They don't even let their kids play with ours. It's as if they think we'll infect them or something! As if our kids aren't as good as their spoilt brats!" one man said.

"You should see how they scare the horses when we go to the shops!" another man cried, jabbing a finger across the expanse. "Then they complain that we're the ones causing a ruckus!"

"They call us thugs and criminals! In front of our children!" yet another added.

The big, tattooed man raised a hand to calm the crowd, though he kept his gaze hard and fixed upon the women. Annabelle's hand bounced against her thigh. Harper remained calm, even in the intimidating presence of the braying men.

"So what?" Harper said, her voice steady and firm. "Do you intend to live like this forever? In a climate of hostility? Will you hold on to your grudges and issues with the villagers or let them go?"

"We didn't start this battle," a man said.

"No one did," Annabelle replied, picking up the baton from Harper. "There were misunderstandings. A simple land issue that—with a little compromise and discussion—could have been dealt with quickly and pleasantly."

Suddenly a lively, high voice called from behind the men. "She's right! Let them through."

CHAPTER THIRTY-FOUR

THE VOICE SEEMED to jar the men, capturing their attention and causing them to look back at the person to whom the voice belonged. They parted slowly, allowing Annabelle and Harper to see an old woman walking towards them. She wobbled as she leant heavily on a knotted, gnarly stick.

"Reverend," the old woman said, smiling wryly as she drew to a stop a few feet from Annabelle and Harper. "We finally meet." Harper looked at Annabelle in confusion.

"You must be Jonquil," Annabelle said, looking the woman directly in the eye.

Jonquil gave her a wide smile, then waved away the men who promptly obeyed, allowing the women to stand in the semicircle alone.

"Your husband was rather rattled after he spoke to me," Jonquil said, a provocative edge to her voice.

"He's not my husband yet," Annabelle replied.

"Soon, though," Jonquil said, chuckling lightly. "Is that why you've come? Are you afraid that the monsters and magic that lurk in this camp might ruin your special day?"

Harper opened her mouth to respond, but Annabelle interrupted her.

"I'm worried that the tension between your camp and the village might cause problems for both of us."

"Hmph!" the old woman snorted derisively. "What could you possibly do to us that you haven't done already? We've been kicked from pillar to post, our children frightened, our men suspected for no reason. Earlier they were accused of pinching a book from a pub. A book, I tell you! What would we want with a book? Tell me how it could be worse."

Annabelle sighed with regret at the woman's defiant words. "There's a lot of tension, and it's rising. There's been a murder in the village and an arson attack. No one's been arrested." Her eyes lit up as a thought struck her. "You could be in as much danger as anyone. It seems that there is some anti-witch sentiment in the air. I believe you identify as a witch, no?"

For a few seconds, Jonquil studied the vicar, her sardonic smile returning as she regarded Annabelle. Finally, she nodded slowly. "You are a good, steadfast woman. There are dark forces at play. More than your people understand. These shadows are seeking, observing, and hiding in plain sight."

"Help us find them then," Harper insisted.

Jonquil turned to Harper, and a dramatic change came over her expression. Something about the pathologist stunned her. After a moment, the old woman stepped forwards slowly, enraptured by her. With a long, knobby, arthritic finger, she reached out to touch Harper's face. Harper did her best not to flinch.

"You . . ." Jonquil whispered slowly, reverently, as she stroked Harper's cheek. Harper stood firm. "It is you who is at the centre of it."

"Centre? Of what?" Annabelle asked.

Slowly, Jonquil pulled back, as if fatigued now by whatever she had seen in Harper. She looked at Annabelle. "I cannot say," the old woman muttered, serious now. She dropped her finger.

Harper shook her head quickly, glad not to be the centre of attention any longer. "When we arrived, one of the men referred to Reverend Annabelle as another preacher. What did he mean? Has someone else visited you before us?"

"The only visitor we've had in days from your village has been your inspector," Jonquil said, bringing a hand to her forehead as if struggling with a headache. "He was probably referring to Neil."

Annabelle and Harper grabbed each other with alarm. "Neil?" Annabelle said.

"Yes," Jonquil answered.

"He came here?"

"He lives here—for now," Jonquil said. She turned slowly, raising an arm to point at a shabby caravan with a dent along the side. It was parked at the edge of the camp. As if on cue, a man appeared in the doorway. He was blond, tall, and pale. Puffy bags like tiny Cornish pasties lay under his eyes. He scratched the back of his head. His unfocused eyes slowly fixed on the women as they stared back at him.

For a few seconds, each was as astounded as the other. Then, before Annabelle's and Harper's thoughts could catch up, Neil leapt down from the caravan. He ran away from the camp, towards the woods behind. Annabelle and Harper swapped the quickest of looks. In a flash, Annabelle set off at a charge, Harper's reactions only a little slower.

Soon, they were chasing Neil with every fibre of their beings, determined to catch him and have things out. Along the side of the field they went, keeping close to the hedgerow where the grass grew, feet pounding against the soft ground. Annabelle lifted her skirts above the long grass that risked tripping her up, her heart thumping from the sudden, unexpected pursuit.

Neil ran desperately, arms flailing. He was a poor runner, his only advantage his lengthy stride. Annabelle, with her long legs and athleticism, closed the gap, but soon the springy grass gave way to the dry soil of the woods, the soft thudding of their feet replaced by the crunch of the woodland as a maze of twisted roots and low branches threatened to obscure the escapee and impede his pursuers. Neil seemed to understand this, for as soon as he was deep enough into the woods, he changed direction, sidestepping tree trunks and darting away from the open areas.

"Where is he?" Harper called to Annabelle. She looked frantically around her.

"This way!" Annabelle called back over her shoulder. She hopped around ancient trees and pushed on through dense bushes in order to keep Neil in sight.

No sooner had she said it, however, than Annabelle lost sight of him. She slapped her hands against a tree to push herself off in a different direction and stumbled onto a path that she could have sworn Neil had taken. But she couldn't see him. She scanned the woods, her eyes whipping around so fast her eyeballs ached, desperate to sight some movement or hear the sound of crunching twigs.

"Ah!" came a cry from behind her. "Annabelle! He's here!"

Annabelle called out, "Harper? Where are you?" She darted towards the sound of Harper's voice.

The pathologist yelped, then cried out. "Over here!"

Annabelle moved even quicker. Emerging from behind

a large tree, she could see far ahead into a small clearing where fallen trunks had long since gathered moss. There, Annabelle saw a sight she dreaded: Neil and Harper engaged in confrontation.

She ran forwards, hoping to get there before Neil gained the upper hand, watching all the while as the pair grappled with a large branch that Neil wielded as a weapon. Harper kicked him, pushing him away with her foot, but losing her grip on the branch. She overbalanced and tripped backwards. She staggered against a log and fell to the ground, the dried leaves of the past winter cushioning her fall with a brief rustle. Neil swung the heavy branch over his head.

Annabelle charged Harper's attacker, her height and speed providing momentum that made up for her lack of strength. The tackle sent both crashing to the ground. They grabbed and pulled at each other, a bundle of clothes and flailing limbs. Annabelle, exhausted from her sprint, found the cloth of her cassock acting like a Chinese finger trap. With every twist, the cassock wrapped itself more tightly around her body, fighting her as determinedly as her assailant.

Annabelle stared up at the blond man's wild blue eyes. She saw fear and anger there. She watched with horror as he raised his fist for a blow that would surely prove painful and braced herself for a horrible, unavoidable fate. Annabelle squeezed her eyes shut and prayed.

She prayed not for herself, but for Harper, and that the pathologist would escape. She prayed that the man towering over her would see His light and never commit such a godless act again. She prayed that her trip to the travellers' camp had not entirely been in vain, that something good would result from it. Then she realised she had been praying a while.

Annabelle opened her eyes to see an arm wrapped around Neil's neck. He was in a headlock. Someone pulled him off her. The thump of a branch landing on the ground reached her ears along with the unmistakable click of handcuffs. A hand gently lifted her to her feet.

"Constable Raven!" she said before noticing the other man who was lifting Neil by his handcuffs. "Mike!"

Mike tried to shoot Annabelle his best "I told you so" look but failed miserably. He turned Neil around to face him. "Thank you both!" she said. Annabelle patted herself down, smoothing her hair like a cat licking its fur.

"No need to thank us, Reverend," Raven said. "It was Dr. Jones here. She did the hard work. We just showed up to the after-party and cleaned up." A few feet away, Harper stood, flushed and huffing.

"My, Harper, how did you do it? I thought I was a goner."

"Oh, it was nothing."

"It was something," Mike argued. "I saw it." Mike shoved Neil towards Raven, who took over the handling of the captive. The inspector walked over to give Annabelle a hug.

"Are you okay?" he mumbled into her shoulder.

"Yes, I'm fine, thank you," Annabelle replied into his. "But . . . how? What . . . ? How come you're here?"

"Did you really think I'd let you two go off alone to see those travellers? When there's a murderer loose?" Mike said. "I followed you with Raven and watched from the woods. I was waiting for something to happen. I knew it would."

Annabelle laughed nervously, anxiety and fright still

crackling around her body. "Gosh, I suppose I'm in the odd position of having to be grateful that you don't trust me," she stuttered, stupefied, still catching her breath.

"Oh, it was never a question of trust, Annabelle," Mike said. "I always have faith"—he winked at her—"that you'll get yourself into trouble eventually."

CHAPTER THIRTY-FIVE

NEIL, HARPER, AND Annabelle sat on a log like naughty schoolchildren. Mike stood in front of them. It wasn't normal protocol, but Mike thought it best to have them all present for a provisional interview. There would be plenty of time for thorough one-on-one interrogations later.

"What's your last name?" he asked the young man opposite him.

Neil's blue eyes flickered nervously to the inspector's face. His hands fidgeted, and his shoulders folded inwards, as if he were trying to make himself as insignificant as possible.

"Hynde," he stuttered, swallowing with effort.

"Neil Hynde," intoned Mike slowly as if familiarising himself with the name. "Well, we've got a lot to go over, Neil Hynde. Where do we start?"

The man quivered and shrugged. "Are you one of the travellers?" Annabelle asked him.

Neil looked at her. "No."

"Then why are you living with them?"

"I came here from Truro. I'm just hiking around looking for work, and I was living in my tent, which gets a bit cold at night this time of year. The travellers found me walking the lanes. They gave me somewhere to stay."

"Why?" Mike asked.

Neil swallowed before answering. "I dunno. Felt sorry for me, I suppose."

"No, I mean why did you come here from Truro? There's more work in the city than there is out here."

"I'm a missionary."

Mike scratched his cheek, then looked at Harper and Annabelle to see if they shared his confusion. "You came from Truro—fifty miles away—to Upton St. Mary as a missionary?" Mike asked, on the verge of laughing.

Neil swallowed again, his wild, fear-filled eyes darting around. "My sword is with the Lord, to be blessed by following justice, and justice alone, to bring light where there is darkness. That is the reason for my earthly presence."

Mike pinched the bridge of his nose and sighed. This was going to be a long one. "And what darkness were you planning to bring to light exactly?" Neil's blue eyes flickered again, then he looked down at the ground. "Go on," Mike said. "Out with it." Everyone watched as Neil's mouth opened but quickly shut again.

Mike folded his arms. "Look, this whole thing is going to unravel with or without you. Your only choice is how easy you make it for yourself. You physically attacked two women—a vicar and a pathologist—for crying out loud. Best get it over with." Mike bent at the waist and put his face three inches from Neil's. There was a degree of menace about Mike's jawline that communicated he was in no mood for fudging, fibbing, or obfuscation. "I've been in this position a hundred times, seen many men and women in the same spot as you, and trust me, the easiest thing is to tell the truth. So tell me: What was it that got you so upset that you came to Upton St. Mary to put it right?"

Neil's breaths were coming quickly, their rhythm jerky, making him bob up and down on the log. It was as if he had something inside his small chest that threatened to escape, something so powerful that he wouldn't so much as speak of it else it would erupt from him of its own accord.

"Her!" he screamed suddenly, punching his thigh with a fist. He pointed at Annabelle with one hand and shielded his eyes with his other to avoid looking at her.

"Me?" Annabelle was aghast. "You came to put me right?"

"Yes!" Neil hissed loudly. "A vicar, the most sacrosanct, privileged, hallowed position on earth in the eyes of the Lord. You make a mockery of it!"

"I do? How?" Annabelle gasped.

"By being a woman!" Neil screamed.

This was all too much for Annabelle—the looming wedding, her concerns about being a good wife, Philippa's nagging, the travellers' threat, murder in her community, the burning of the marquee. It was a lot. And now she was being accused of . . . just being! She was as offended as she'd ever been in her life. She stood up. "I beg your pardon?" she shouted.

"An imposter!" Neil also stood. They were nose to nose. "A fraud! A symbol of everything wrong with the church! Modernity! You drag the divine into the gutter with your so-called progressiveness!"

"How dare you!" Annabelle bellowed, spreading her fists out wide. "What on God's holy earth gives you the right to question my ability to serve the Lord?"

"I have more rights than you'll ever have. I'm a man!"

"Oh, really? Well, as a woman, I have done more to serve my community in the name of God than you have ever done!"

"I don't care if you've walked on water, fed the five thousand, and raised the dead! You're still a woman!"

"'There's no Jew or Greek, servant or free, male or female: because we are all one in Jesus Christ.' Galatians three twenty-eight!"

"'But I permit not a woman to teach, nor to have dominion over a man, but to be in quietness.' Timothy two twelve!"

"Stop it!" Mike bellowed loudly. "Both of you!"

CHAPTER THIRTY-SIX

MIKE SHOVED NEIL back onto the log and gently pressed Annabelle's shoulder for her to sit down as well. The two sat, glaring ahead, red-faced and breathless. Harper moved to sit closer to Annabelle. She put a soothing hand on her shoulder.

"Let's just calm down a little, shall we?" Mike said "Crikey." He adjusted his collar. He was sweating. "So, you don't like women priests, eh?" Neil glowered quietly but seemed out of words after his outburst.

"Presumably," Harper said, stepping in as Annabelle calmed down, "that was why you razed the marquee to the ground."

Neil glanced to one side. He looked a little embarrassed. "I didn't mean to do that. It was an accident."

"An accident?" Mike said. "How exactly do you set fire to a large, empty tent in the middle of a big lawn accidentally?"

Neil closed his eyes and inhaled several times. He appeared to be meditating. Mike leant forwards to give him a prod. Neil's eyes opened. "I had written a message for . . .

her." He scowled at Annabelle again. Annabelle's nostrils flared. "It was a large poster explaining all the ways in which her hubris and fakery are an affront to the sanctity of the church. You're a sham, a con artist, a pretender, an imposter!" Harper squeezed Annabelle's arm tight to stop her from barking a response.

"Go on," Mike urged.

"I wanted to pin it to the marquee so that the guests would see it on your wedding day. When I went to do it, though, there were too many people around. There was the gardener, some people playing croquet, and also the owners." Neil shook his head like he was trying to dislodge a fly from his hair. "Godless, female creatures walking around chattering in their heathen manner." Harper felt Annabelle tense.

"Let's just stick to what happened, okay?" Mike urged, eyeing Annabelle carefully as he assessed her emotional temperature. It was high, feverish even. "Don't get carried away now."

"I hid in the nearby woods, behind a tree, and waited there until I was sure everyone had gone. It took a long time, but the Lord blessed me with patience that day."

Annabelle rolled her eyes and tutted. The inspector tried not to smirk. Neil was insulting many of Annabelle's most fondly cherished values, and she was having none of it. It was what he loved about her. Her steadfastness, some might call it stubbornness, in the face of provocation and mistrust.

"It was night by the time I could perform my sacred act without being seen," Neil continued. "Deep in the night. Very dark, as is wont for such places of sin. I stumbled through the darkness, barely able to see a few feet in front of me. I prayed for Him to show me, to guide me, to make me

His tool, His servant. But I tripped over a tent peg and fell into the marquee." Annabelle gasped. Harper's eyebrows shot up. Mike covered his mouth and briefly closed his eyes.

"I remembered that I had a lighter," Neil said. "And I found the entrance to the marquee. I went inside. But the lighter got hot and burned my finger." Neil held up his thumb to show a large and rather painful-looking blister. Mike's hand wandered from his mouth to his forehead. "So I pulled my sleeve over my hand to protect it from the heat . . ."

"Oh, Lord," Harper muttered quietly.

"I was unfolding the poster when I realised I could smell burning. I looked down and saw that my sleeve was on fire. The devil had tricked me, sent me astray, I thought! I prayed quickly as I tore off my coat and my top and threw them to the ground. In my panic, they landed against the tent walls. 'What satanic trap is this?' I thought. The tent quickly became an inferno, an earthly hell around me! I ran outside—by now, it was well ablaze —and went back to my hiding place in the woods. I watched as the forces of evil did their work, destroying it. But then I realised that it was all part of His plan. He was sending a message far more profound and visceral than my notice could ever have achieved. He was proving me right."

Annabelle opened her mouth to object, but a fierce look from Mike quietened her.

"I couldn't leave," Neil said, so lost in his tale that he ignored those around him. "The Lord's message still had to be delivered directly. I couldn't risk it being lost. My poster had been taken by the flames, so I pulled a page from a notebook I carry and wrote the first thing that came to mind. No dwelling shall hide the woman from her own evil. I trusted that the Lord would ensure the person who read it understood."

"What had you written on the poster?" Harper asked.

"Several hundred words, some quotes she should reread from the Bible." Neil glared at Annabelle, who glared back.

"Several hundred words on a poster?" Mike repeated, whistling. "And instead, you had to make do with just a few words on a scrap of notepaper. Must have annoyed you."

Neil stared at the inspector without fear now. "The Lord guides me, and I have faith in his plan."

Mike and Annabelle exchanged glances, taking a moment to digest the outlandish—yet somehow believable—story of how Neil had turned an objection to women priests into a spot of arson. "Alright," Mike said. "So, you came from Truro to Upton St. Mary to correct what you saw as the grand injustice of the village church having a female vicar. And you stayed with the travellers..."

"They are poor, harmless," Neil quickly explained, his anxiety now replaced by righteousness.

"Poor, certainly, but harmless isn't a word I'd use to describe them," Mike said.

Neil straightened and stuck out his small chest as he prepared to deliver his defence of the travellers. "They live as the Lord decreed, from the land, without material concerns. They are sinners, absolutely, but aren't we all? And as were many of those with whom Jesus communed."

"I see now, 'a den of sin,'" Mike said. "But we've not broached the other reason we want to talk to you, Neil. The reason we've been searching for you. The murder of Kathleen Webster."

The certainty with which Neil had expressed himself over his religious beliefs evaporated. The confident man was replaced by a confused one. "What? I don't understand," he said.

Mike took a deep breath as he realised Neil wasn't going to make this easy. "The murder of Kathleen Webster. Tell me how and why you did it."

"B-but I didn't," Neil stuttered, his glance turning wild again as he looked at Mike. "I didn't kill anyone!"

"Listen, Neil, we know that you did it. We know that you worked on the Webster sisters' property a week before the murder."

"B-but that's ridiculous! You can't honestly be accusing me of killing her. Why would I do that?"

"We also know that they sacked you. And now we know," Mike said, looking at Annabelle, "that you can't stand women."

"No! I didn't kill anyone! Murder is a sin!"

"Really?" Mike said in a loud, commanding voice. "And standing over my future wife with your fist raised isn't?"

CHAPTER THIRTY-SEVEN

"THAT WAS DIFFERENT!" Neil cried. "I panicked! I had no intention of hurting her!"

"Could've fooled me!"

"And what about me?" Harper said diffidently. "It certainly seemed like you intended to hurt me with that branch you were wielding."

"I-I-I just wanted to scare you! I wanted you both to leave me alone! With the Lord as my witness, I would never have hurt you! And I certainly didn't kill anyone! Please! Oh, dear Lord, have mercy." Neil leant over, his elbows on his knees, a vein in his neck throbbing beneath his flushed skin. His voice shook.

Annabelle got up from the log and walked over to Mike. "Mike," Annabelle whispered in his ear. "Could I have a word?"

Mike looked at her calm, blank expression, then back at the terrified man.

"Okay, Neil. Take a little time to let the act wear off, okay?" Mike said. He, Harper, and Annabelle walked away, leaving Raven to guard their prisoner.

Out of Neil's earshot, Harper looked serious, businesslike. Annabelle, her cheeks flushed pink, hopped from one foot to the other. Mike folded his arms, satisfied with how the conversation with Neil had gone. "What do you think?" he asked the women.

Harper shook her head. "I don't know what to think. He sounds a bit messed up to me. But there are a lot of strange people around. Doesn't mean they're murderers. But then again . . ."

"I believe him," Annabelle said.

Mike knit his brow. "What?"

"I believe him," Annabelle repeated. "I don't think he murdered Kathleen."

It took a few seconds for Mike to convince himself he had heard her correctly. "Annabelle, the guy is a lunatic! He was just shouting at you across a log like a madman. He's capable of anything! I'd be surprised if Kathleen Webster is the only person he's killed!"

Annabelle sighed and shook her head. "I don't actually think he's that bad," she said, ignoring Mike's snort of incredulity. "Misguided, perhaps. A little passionate, but I don't think he's capable of murder."

"He burned down the marquee!" Mike cried. "The marquee for our wedding!"

"By accident," Annabelle retorted. "He only wanted to pin up a message; rather harmless, when you think about it."

"Who's to say he didn't kill Kathleen Webster by accident too?" Mike said, still astonished at the fact he was having this argument. "Perhaps he brought her a cup of tea and somehow skewered her to the floor! Sorry, Harper."

"He would have admitted it, I think, if that was the case," Annabelle said. "He admitted the marquee incident was his fault."

"The devil's fault, remember?" Harper added. "And then he made as though it was God's plan all along."

"I genuinely think if he killed Kathleen Webster, he would admit it. He has faith, Mike, and I understand faith. He is very committed, even if we disagree in our interpretation of it. His faith is strong enough that he wouldn't fear the consequences if he felt that what he was doing was right."

Mike rubbed his face roughly, suddenly feeling tired and frustrated so soon after the triumph of finding the suspect he had been seeking. He wanted to put this case to bed. He had things to do, a wedding to prepare for, a woman—this woman—to marry.

"You call that faith?" he said. "He's in there calling you an imposter, a charlatan, and you think that's his faith talking?"

"Those of us who ask for open minds mustn't stop trying to understand."

"What about the attack? Do you really expect me to believe he attacked you by accident?"

"I think he was desperate and acting out of character."

"He has a thing against women, women priests in particular, and you think acting violently towards them is out of character?" Mike shook his head, struggling to accept Annabelle's ideas were even worthy of consideration, let alone believable. "The man over there is a killer if ever I saw one! You couldn't find a more homicidal personality!" They all glanced over to appraise Neil. He looked very small and anxious. Not at all like a murderous maniac. "Harper, back me up here, will you?"

"Yes, what do you think, Harper?" Annabelle asked. She and Mike looked at the pathologist, keenly awaiting her objective, cool view as if she were the referee determining the result of a boxing match. Harper took a deep breath, cast her eyes across the field, and answered only after she had considered the situation carefully.

"The possibility that he is the murderer is undeniable," she said calmly. "But at the same time, there's no evidence. He seems willing to cooperate considering he admits to burning down the marquee, and he seems an open book about almost everything he's done—good or bad. He doesn't appear to be cunning or even terribly competent. Does he even know about the connection between witches and pitchforks?"

Mike growled and clenched his teeth. "So, what am I supposed to do now? Go out and look for another suspect when the most likely one is right here? I've got nothing to go on! We've scoured the crime scene. Our only witness, Joan, is about as comprehensible as the ingredients label on a box of Froot Loops, and about as sensible. Sorry again, Harper. And . . . and . . . you won't even let me interrogate the travellers!"

There was a rustle in the bushes behind Annabelle. Mike looked over and saw a big man on an even bigger horse amongst the trees. It was Dylan, the bear-man from the travellers' camp. He was riding bareback, holding ropes for reins. The two men locked gazes. The horse trotted sideways, Dylan tightening his reins to keep control. Mike's eyes narrowed as he assessed the threat. And then, Dylan gave the horse a nudge with his heels. The horse cantered off. When they disappeared from view, they left no sign they had been there. Mike wondered if he had imagined them.

He turned back to the women. "Look, I can't keep this Neil in custody for very long. Arson will get downgraded to an accidental fire charge as soon as the court sees what a blundering fool this guy is, and by the looks of it, neither of you is willing to stick an assault charge on him!"

"Mike," Annabelle said in a soft voice. She placed her hands on his arms. He looked at her dolefully, his face filled with disappointment and fatigue. "You can't arrest a man without evidence. Even if you feel sure. You know that."

Mike looked at his fiancée and sighed regretfully. "I know," he said. He sounded defeated. "But we're getting married the day after tomorrow, Annabelle. I don't want to get married with such a messy, gruesome case playing on my mind. I want it done. Over. I want to go on honeymoon with the case all tied up, preferably in handcuffs."

"Why don't you get another detective to take over?" Harper said.

Mike looked at her. "That call from Truro before I left the station was to tell me they don't have anyone available. If I don't find the murderer by the time we walk down the aisle, they'll get away with it. The trail will have gone cold by the time we return. And that won't make me happy. Not happy at all."

Annabelle searched the face of her husband-to-be, a face she now knew so well and yet still wanted to look at for the rest of her days. Forlornly, she gazed at Neil, a man who had shouted in her face, who bore her ill will, who deemed her entire existence an affront. A man she still felt sympathy for, a man she wanted to help. She said, "I understand all that, but it is better to serve no justice at all than to cede injustice."

CHAPTER THIRTY-EIGHT

THEY TRUDGED BACK to the cars. Raven and Neil led the way, followed by Annabelle and Harper. Mike brought up the rear. They walked in silence as they meandered through trees, along hedgerows, and across fields, the distance surprising the two women who hadn't realised how far they had run. They avoided the travellers' camp, keeping it to their left with woods in between them as they navigated the gentle downwards slope of a hill.

The sun was setting. Annabelle pulled her sleeves over her hands to keep them warm and watched where she put her feet, the ground changing and uneven. She was deep in thought. Every so often, she let out a deep sigh and rubbed her face. Harper was weary too, the effects of the chase, the fight, and her grief finally draining her.

Behind them, Mike was equally thoughtful. It was unlikely now that the case would be closed before the wedding. As he thought about it, he winced and made a sucking sound with his cheek. There was no way around it. Annabelle was right; he couldn't rush to judge a case that wasn't roundly supported with evidence or a confession. Dejectedly, he let out his own big sigh.

He heard a noise behind him and looked over his shoulder to see the huge black horse he'd noticed earlier in the trees. It was cantering towards him, Dylan on its back. Dylan steered the horse to within a few feet of Mike, its black coat glistening despite the fading sun, its mane and tail falling long and loose. The horse had hooves as big as Mike's head, and with more hair. The horse was easily a foot taller than the inspector, with withers and shoulders that would crush him should he be unfortunate enough to find himself between them and another solid object. Up close, the horse was a terrifying, if magnificent, sight.

Mike refused to stop moving, and Dylan and the horse fell into a walk beside him. "What do you want?" Mike said.

"You should listen to her." Dylan nodded ahead to Annabelle. "She's got her head on straight."

"Oh yeah? How would you know?"

"I can just tell. You don't deserve her. Wouldn't be surprised if she wakes up in time and jilts you at the altar." Dylan leered, showing an impressive array of black and yellow teeth.

"Look, have you got something to say that's of any use? Because if not, clear off. And if you're just here to hurl insults, also clear off. I'm not in the mood."

"We don't like it when you come around for no reason."

Mike pulled up short. "What? No reason? I could have you arrested for half a dozen crimes if I chose to. You'd better watch your step, or I'll get a warrant to search your camp. See if you like that!"

"And search for what?"

"An old notebook for starters. And I'm sure I can come with some more ideas if I need to."

"There's no notebook at the camp or anywhere to do with us. You're barking up the wrong tree." Dylan pulled sharply on his rope reins and the horse stopped, throwing its head back and dancing sideways two steps. Dylan pulled on his left rein and dug in with his left heel. The horse turned around to face the opposite direction. "Don't come around no more, d'you hear?"

"Don't give me reason."

"We're a peaceful people, but we look after our own and won't have outsiders telling us what to do."

Mike put his hands on his hips. "The law's the law." He wagged his finger. "And I'm watching you lot."

"And we're watching you." Dylan gave the restless horse a kick with both heels. It shot off, galloping down the side of the woods until Mike could see them no more. He tutted and blew out his cheeks, swinging around to catch up with the others even more dejected than he'd been before Dylan's visit. An unresolved case, a hostile community, and anxieties about his fiancée, who he suspected was keeping something from him, was not how he had planned to spend the run-up to his wedding.

CHAPTER THIRTY-NINE

THEY PARKED THE cars outside the police station.

"Annabelle, I can still drive you home. Raven will take care of Mr. Hynde here," Mike said.

"Thanks, but I'm going to hang around the village for a bit. There's someone I want to see."

"Okay, see you later." Mike disappeared inside.

"What are you going to do now, Annabelle?" Harper said.

"I don't know, to be honest. Wander around for a bit. Collect my thoughts."

"Fancy an ice cream?" Harper nodded across the road to an ice cream van. Right on cue, the notes of the van's jingle, the bane of every parent's existence, pealed through the air, calling the children like a modern-day pied piper.

"Why not? I think we deserve one after the afternoon we've had."

"Afternoon, Vicar. What can I get you?" Mr. Trilby said. He was a small man, slight and short, a jockey in his early days and the perfect size for the limited space of his van. He certainly didn't appear to eat his profits by indulging in his stock.

Annabelle looked at the side of his van. "Ooh, there's such a lot to choose from!"

"How about a hedgehog?"

"No, thanks, Mr. Trilby. Lovely creatures but full of fleas."

"Nah, not those kinds of hedgehogs. Here, let me get you one. My treat."

Annabelle watched as Mr. Trilby took a cone and topped it with ice cream. Instead of handing it to her though, he leant into a fridge. "What are you doing, Mr. Trilby?"

"I'm covering the ice cream with lovely Cornish clotted cream, my dear. Lovely. Now we top it off with chocolate." He dipped the clotted-cream-covered ice cream into a vat of melted milk chocolate. "And finish off with nuts." He rolled the chocolate across a plate strewn with chopped almonds. "There you go!" He handed Annabelle the biggest ice cream she had ever seen. "No charge. Early wedding present. Enjoy yourself! Don't blame me if you can't get in your dress on Saturday!" The small man laughed.

Annabelle and Harper, who'd gone for a more modest fruit lolly, wandered along the high street, sucking and licking their treats until they reached a bench. "Let's sit. I need to take the weight off my knees," Annabelle said. "They took a beating this afternoon." They sat down, obscuring the plaque that commemorated the life of Charity Boniface, the elderly lollipop lady who had ensured that Upton St. Mary schoolchildren crossed the road safely for nigh on sixty years until old age and good living finally took her to the Lord. It was Charity's dying wish to be buried with her lollipop, and Annabelle had seen to it. She'd had to ask the bishop.

"Hello, ladies. Waiting for me?" Dr. Whitefield said. He was arriving for evening surgery.

"Oh no, Dr. Whitefield. We're just taking a breather," Annabelle said. "Long day."

"Ah yes, wedding prep. When my daughter got married, I didn't see my wife for weeks!" Dr. Whitefield turned his attention to Harper. "I say, are you Joan Penberthy's niece?"

"Yes, I am. Harper Jones."

Annabelle introduced them. "This is Dr. Whitefield, our local vet."

"I'm sorry for your loss, my dear. Kathleen was a fine woman. You stay here. I'll get Sooty for you. No need to get up."

"Wh . . .?" Harper said, but Dr. Whitefield disappeared into his surgery. A few minutes later, he came out with a cat basket.

"Here you go. No charge. Not in the circumstances."

"But who is this?" Harper looked inside the basket to see two golden eyes staring at her unblinkingly amidst a big ball of black fluff.

"Why, this is Sooty, of course. Your aunt's cat. Your aunts were worried about her when I paid them a visit to see to their poorly goat a few days ago. I took Sooty to stay with me for a bit to see what was wrong. Gave her some medication and she's as right as rain now. I've called Joan a few times but, well, I'm sure it's all a bit much for her at the moment."

"So, the cat has been here with you all this time? Well, I never. That's another mystery solved."

"Take good care of her. Now, I must get on, ladies. Have

a good evening. See you in church, Annabelle!" Dr. Whitefield lumbered off.

"You've got yourself a new pet, Harper," Annabelle laughed. She'd never seen Harper as a cat person, but Harper stuck her finger through the front of the cat basket and was making squeaking noises.

"I suppose I have," Harper said. "I'd better get over to the farm. Aunt Joan will be pleased to see Sooty—if she remembers she has a cat, that is."

"Bye, Harper." Annabelle waved as her friend strolled off, carrying her basket in one hand, her ice lolly in another. In the distance, she saw the unmistakeable bulk of Father John coming towards her.

"Annabelle! Good grief, that's a big ice cream." Father John walked up to her.

"Isn't it just? I'm starting to feel a little sick to be honest."

"Any luck with the notebook?" Father John sat down on the bench.

"We didn't find it, but we did find the person who burned down the marquee. It was an accident, not arson. Not purposeful arson, anyway."

"That's a shame about the journal. I wonder what happened to it." Father John looked up at the sky, then regarded Annabelle curiously. "You're looking a little tired. How are you? Ready for the wedding? Not long now."

Finally defeated by the ice cream, Annabelle wrapped the rest in a napkin and tossed it in a bin. She leant her elbow on the arm of the bench and propped her head on her fist. "To be honest, Father, I don't even want to think about it."

CHAPTER FORTY

ANNABELLE SHUT HER eyes so tightly that she saw stars when she opened them. "I'm tired, and fed up, and . . ." She exhaled and started to pick at a splinter in the bench. "Oh, I don't know. It should be the best day of my life, but I feel such pressure."

Father John scooted over and put his arm around Annabelle's shoulders. "And which part of getting married is bothering you so? The wedding, the marriage, or your choice of husband?"

"Not my choice of husband. Not at all. I'm very sure about that. It's the wedding. I feel 'on show,' and that's not where I like to be."

Father John smiled. "You mean like you're not on show every Sunday from a pulpit five feet off the floor?"

"You know what I mean. I'm in my element in the pulpit. I'm made for the pulpit. I mean as a bride. All the primping and pressing, preparing and proving. I feel like a loaf of bread being pummelled into shape. Philippa's got me down for something called a mani-pedi!" Father John laughed.

"What should I do, Father? I find myself anxious, unable to focus on the wedding preparations. I'm keeping everyone dangling whilst they wait for me to make decisions. I'm not being fair. I've prayed, I've asked for a sign, but nothing is forthcoming. I don't know what to do. I'm worried I'll be a letdown. And . . . and everyone's involved. How on earth will I repay them?"

"With your love, Annabelle, with your love."

"Eh?"

"The villagers are merely reciprocating all the love you've shown them over the years. Doing this for you, experiencing it with you, makes them happy. Your happiness is their repayment. They'll give you and Mike a liftoff that's powerful and magnetic. Embrace their energy; let their love for you carry you forth into the union that will last the rest of your life."

"But . . . but . . ."

"But?"

"It's not just the wedding," Annabelle said. "It's marriage. I feel I'm simply not cut out for it."

"Oh, Annabelle . . . Come now."

"I'm serious. I'm quite sure no one's ever looked at me and thought 'good marriage material.' I worship the Lord and cake, not always in that order. I'm a clodhopping, cack-handed, cat-loving vicar who loves her congregation and celebrates the human condition in all its craziness and inconsistency largely because I'm like that too. I know I've been blessed in my life so far. I've been able to do so many things that bring me so much satisfaction: helping people, praising God, serving a wonderful community. I feel confident and comfortable doing that. I do love Mike so very much. He adds even more joy and substance to my life. I can't envision a future without him."

"But?"

"Will I be a good policeman's wife? Will he get fed up with me, with my faults, fussiness, and foibles? Can I serve everyone well without feeling like I'm doing a poor job across the board? And don't even get me started on motherhood! When I think of being a wife and all that entails I . . . I honestly don't know if I'm up to it."

Mrs. Penhaligon walked by. She pushed her wheeled shopping basket ahead of her, a baguette sticking out like a warning. The trolley was one of a fleet that Annabelle had raised money for to make the lives of the elderly in the village a little easier. Mrs. Penhaligon blinked at Annabelle and raised a hand.

Father John allowed the moment to stand, his hand poised to bring Annabelle a tissue should the quiver in her voice turn to sobs. Eventually, Annabelle took several deep breaths and relaxed her shoulders. "Do you want me to tell you the big secret of marriage, Annabelle? The thing no one thinks to tell you but which everyone who marries learns eventually?"

Annabelle took in Father John's warm smile and nodded. "A wedding is a celebration, a confirmation, a ritual. It's a wonderful thing. It marks the end of one life and the start of a new one. A difference that is significant. But nothing much changes," he said slowly. Annabelle looked at him, entranced by his words. "Not in the short-term or on the surface."

"What do you mean?"

"One week after your wedding, you—and Mike—will be the same people you were a week before it. Marriage doesn't make domesticated servants or nagging cronies of women who weren't before. Neither does it make selfish layabouts of men who were once hardworking and considerate. And certainly not of people like you and Mike, who are steady and true.

"And in the long-term?"

"Certain things change over the years. There'll be times when you're at your best and Mike isn't and vice versa. Your circumstances will alter, forcing you to draw upon your strengths, fortitude, and determination. But what you will hold on to at that point is your love, your shared values, your common goals. With those, and persistence and flexibility, you'll get through. And as long as you have been honest about whatever 'faults and foibles' you bring to the marriage . . ."

"No hiding them," Annabelle snorted.

" . . . then you can be sure that Mike has accepted you for who you are and loves you because of them, or perhaps despite them. Marriage is about the blending of your different strengths and being willing to work as a team, and you know all about that. Just look at you and Philippa!" Annabelle snorted again.

"Annabelle, you're doing a wonderful thing. You're giving the gift of love to everyone. Lead the way with your head held high. You've given so much; now allow yourself to receive." Father John silently closed his hand over Annabelle's. She had worried a hole in the bench the size of a ten pence piece.

"Look, perhaps the answer is right in front of you."

"But I can't see it!"

"And why is that, Annabelle? 'There are none so blind as those who will not see.' What are you resisting? Think on that. Pray. Remember God loves you. Mike too."

CHAPTER FORTY-ONE

ANNABELLE MOVED TO the front of her church and rearranged the candles on the altar table. She looked up at the stained glass window, the moonlight animating its jewelled tones, inviting her thoughts to wander with them. She walked to the intricately sculpted pulpit, stroking the medieval stone depictions of biblical figures, wondering about the lives of those who had worked on them all those years ago, offering their service to an all-loving God. Finally, she sat down in the front pew and, after a short prayer, sat in contemplation.

"Annabelle?" It was Mike. "I wondered if you might be here. Are you alright?" Annabelle budged up and he sat beside her.

"Yes, I'm fine. Just having a few final moments of solitude before the madness ensues."

Mike half stood. "Would you like me to leave?"

"No, no." She patted the pew. "Sit down. There's something I want to tell you."

"Yes?"

"Look, I know I should have said this before, but . . ."

"Yes?"

"It's about the village."

Mike groaned. "That person's not been shoving naughty catalogues in brown paper bags under your door again, have they? I can ask around down the pub, you know. Find out who it is and have a word."

"No, no, it's not that."

"What is it then?"

"It's . . . it's . . ."

Mike leant forwards. "Yes?" Annabelle searched for the words as her thoughts swam around her brain. "Annabelle, look, you can tell me. If it's something embarrassing, I'm sure I've heard worse. If it's a problem, I'm sure we can work it out. If it's last-minute nerves, we can run away and be by ourselves. But if it's"—Mike took a deep breath—"that you've changed your mind, I'm not sure there's anything I can do about that."

Annabelle's eyes widened. "Oh no. No, no, no, no, no. It's nothing like that."

"Well, what is it then?"

Annabelle took a deep breath. "I want you to know that if your job requires us to move to Truro, then I will do so. I can find another parish. Start again."

"Move to Truro?"

"Yes."

"Okay."

"But I-I . . ." Annabelle screwed her eyes up tight. The words came out in a rush. "I really want to live in Upton St. Mary. Like, forever."

"Okay."

"I love it here. I love everything about it. I love the people, and the countryside, the flowers and the birds, and driving the lanes, and the animals, the life and the routines, and the births and the deaths, and other peoples' marriages, the connectedness, the community, even the nosiness, and the gossip, and the interfering, and the lack of privacy . . ." Annabelle was out of breath.

Mike took Annabelle's face in his hands. "Annabelle, look at me." Annabelle regarded him with big eyes. Her heart was pounding. "I said okay."

"W-What? B-But . . ."

"It's okay. I want to live here too. With you."

"Oh."

"Is that what this is all about? All this evasion, procrastination, chasing men through fields, winding Philippa up until she's practically willing to carry out a murder herself?"

"I-I just thought that with your career, that promotion you mentioned, I'd have to move to the city."

"What? Why-ever did you think that? You don't think I'd give up having the Dog and Duck as my local, do you? Have you seen the pubs in Truro?"

"You mean I can stay living in Upton St. Mary, amongst my congregation?"

"Not only that, but I may also put it in our wedding vows. You know, under the 'obey' part! I mean, end our walks? Have the dogs live in a city? Not bloody likely."

"Oh." Annabelle sat back in her seat. A small smile flitted across her face. Oh.

"I'm unlikely to solve this case before the wedding now, so the promotion thing is probably moot anyway."

"There's still a day left. Anything could happen."

"Nah, I think they've got away with it. Tomorrow I'll have to write my report and leave the case for when I come back. By then, the trail will have gone cold. There won't be much chance of apprehending the murderer then." Mike sighed and ran his hand through his hair, leaving it sticking up in a way Annabelle always found attractive.

"So, your promotion . . ."

"Dead in the water would be my guess." He reached out and took her hand. "You'll be married to an ordinary copper for a while yet."

Annabelle felt his thick, strong fingers under her slender, delicate ones. She squeezed his hand. "Suits me."

"Was there anything else?"

"No, no. Carry on."

"So, we're alright?"

"Yes, let's forget I said anything."

They both sat back in the pew, quiet as the mice that Biscuit took care of, the only sound the creak of the ancient pew beneath them. Mike watched the candles on the altar flicker, but he didn't fail to notice the long sigh that Annabelle let out as her eyes briefly closed. Oh.

It was almost midnight when Annabelle crossed the church courtyard to her cottage, the only accompaniment to the moon's subtle light a yellowish glow pouring from the windows. She paused a moment to look at her home, considered the elderly woman who was waiting for her inside, and sighed with regret.

Annabelle let herself in and peered into the living room. Sure enough, Philippa was there, sitting alone on the couch. She was surrounded by elegant, lavender-coloured lace bags filled with small gifts. They lay everywhere—on the cushions next to her, around her feet. She'd even laid rows of them along the back and arms of the sofa. In her lap was a pile of empty bags and boxes of the items with which she was filling them. When Annabelle came into the room, Philippa glanced up with tired eyes.

"Hello," Philippa said. Her face was pale, her eyes weary and bleak.

Annabelle took off her coat and lay it over the back of a chair. Without a word, she moved the lavender bags to the table and settled herself beside Philippa on the sofa. As Philippa watched her sit down, Annabelle leant over and gave her a hug.

"What was that for?" Philippa said.

"For being a wonderful friend. For doing all of this," Annabelle said, gesturing at the bags around them. "And for putting up with me, horrible me, these past few days."

"Hmm," Philippa said, lost for words and still slightly befuddled, but too tired to work things out.

"Honestly, I don't know how you've managed to keep everything together, what with me neglecting everything."

"Well, it's not been easy, let me tell you that!" Philippa chided softly. "I think I should go on the honeymoon with you! I've always wanted to go to—Never mind."

Annabelle laughed gently before looking down. "I think the villagers were right. I was getting cold feet for a while there. It's rather daunting. A massive change. Being a wife, no longer independent, not quite as free to go where I want, when I want, without consideration for another. I wasn't sure I was cut out for it. But now I am. And I'm determined to make it up to you. Just tell me what you need me to do."

Philippa looked around at the bags. "Well, you've left it pretty late. We've only got one more day. I've filled about half of these goodie bags. I was planning to finish the rest tomorrow but, wait a moment, what about the murder? Is that all sorted?"

Annabelle sighed. "Unfortunately not. But I can't

justify delaying my wedding preparations any longer." She slapped her thighs, stood up, and smiled. "Now, we should both get some sleep. You stay here tonight, and we'll get cracking first thing tomorrow morning."

Philippa looked up at the lively Annabelle and smiled. "That sounds like a good plan to me."

CHAPTER FORTY-TWO

EARLY THE NEXT morning, after the briefest of breakfasts, Annabelle and Philippa were back to their harmonious, energetic best. They were two whirlwinds, bustling about each other and communicating almost telepathically as they set to the tasks in hand. Or at least the tasks on Philippa's very long list.

Before the sun had even fully risen on the green lawns around the church, they had already packed the remainder of the gift bags and delivered them to Mr. Malik, the owner of the local shop. He would take them to Gabriella and Sophie at Woodlands Manor. They had also hammered out a strict schedule for the proceedings, from wake-up to the time the DJ would leave, and decided on the hymns for the service and the music to be played at the reception.

"Right," Annabelle said, clapping her hands. "Next port of call is Flynn's, where I am once and for all going to settle the matter of the wedding cake and sweets."

"Annabelle, I think your dress is more important. We should do that first."

"Nuh-uh, Philippa. The dessert choices are crucial to the wedding's success. You know how I am—a connoisseur of, and a glutton for, anything sweet. After years of the parishioners dropping off their gifts of cakes, biscuits, and chocolates, they are going to expect something special from me. I've decided to invite the whole village to the wedding, and that provides me with an opportunity to reciprocate their generosity. I plan to do so with abandon and with cake!" Philippa rolled her eyes but conceded Annabelle's priorities. Mostly she was delighted to have this new, enthusiastic bride-to-be taking interest in her wedding.

"Vicar! I was expecting you. You're just in time! We'll be setting the ovens to warm in just a few minutes." Katie Flynn took Annabelle into the back of the tea shop to pore over yet more samples. Katie was very serious about her baking and brought the intensity of a sommelier to the tasting.

"Hmmm, I think the lavender and lime, the apple and raspberry, and the cherry. I'll take hot chocolate bombs for the children. They'll calm them down after Mr. Trilby has done his stuff making them ice cream hedgehogs from his van."

Next, Annabelle considered the flavour of the wedding cake, treating the decision with great seriousness, almost as if it were life-altering, which of course, to her, it was. "I just think a strawberry mousse layer is too provocative, too outlandish," Annabelle said, tapping her chin. "I'd like my cake to be enjoyed by everyone, and strawberry is far too risky, in my opinion."

Philippa and Katie exchanged a tense glance. "But you said chocolate is too conservative," Katie said. "And it's rare for wedding cakes to involve chocolate anyway."

"It is conservative," Annabelle insisted. "Too ordinary. I want"—she licked her lips—"panache!"

"What about vanilla?" Philippa suggested.

"Vanilla!" Annabelle exclaimed, horrified. She slammed her hands on the table, sending clouds of flour up into the air. "Vanilla!"

"Sorry, Annabelle," Philippa said, shrinking a little. "I just thought . . ."

"No," Annabelle said, suddenly searching forcefully amongst Katie's cupboards. "It should be unique, but not too rarefied. Surprising, but not shocking. People will have high expectations of me—anything less than sensational, than ingenious, than magnificent, and I'll never live it down!"

"It's just a cake, Reverend," Philippa implored, hardly able to believe that she was now trying to calm down Annabelle's enthusiasm. "I'm sure that—"

"What's this?" interrupted Annabelle as she sniffed at a tin of powder.

"That?" Katie said, peering to see what Annabelle was holding. "Oh, that's white chocolate powder."

Annabelle's eyes widened, and a second later, so did her grin.

"White chocolate!" she said. "Yes! White chocolate! And . . . And . . ." She snapped her fingers, searching for something that was on the tip of her tastebuds.

"Lemon?" Katie volunteered hesitantly. "Not too much, just a little. A spring wedding, white chocolate and lemon?" Inwardly, Katie hoped for a positive response. She made an error ordering her last batch of lemon extract and had got stuck with three gallons of it.

Annabelle marched towards Katie Flynn, slammed the tin down, and clutched her by her shoulders. She stared into the baker's face, her eyes shining. "By God!" Annabelle exclaimed. "That's it!"

Half-frightened, half-awestruck, but mostly relieved, Katie nodded. "White chocolate and lemon it is, Vicar."

Annabelle let Katie go and strode to the door. "Thank you, Katie!" she called over her shoulder. "We will leave you in peace to work your magic! I leave the decoration of such a fine cake in your very capable hands!"

Philippa and Katie exchanged glances. Philippa shrugged before Annabelle grabbed her arm, and she quickly scurried after the rampaging reverend.

With the cakes sorted, the two women turned their attention to the flowers. Mrs. Applebury was arranging them. She had been the church florist for twenty-one years. Annabelle and Philippa considered her suggestions, choosing the blend of colours (lavender, pink, and white) and the combination of blooms in season (roses, sweet peas, freesias, peonies, hydrangeas, and lily of the valley) that would make up Annabelle's bouquet, the church decorations and displays, and reception table centrepieces. The flowers had been grown by green-fingered villagers, seeded to bloom at the perfect time for this precise purpose. Village life being what it is, this had kicked off a competition between the growers over whose flowers would be chosen to feature in Annabelle's wedding bouquet. Rivalries had been as fierce and furious as those that took place annually over the growing of the marrow that would win "biggest vegetable" at the St. Mary's church fête. It was not a situation that contributed to sleepy village life in the least, but it was as traditional and customary as the ringing of the church bells to announce the winner had been chosen.

After that, they were off again.

CHAPTER FORTY-THREE

THERE WAS A brief visit to Ted Lovesey at the garage to check on the car that would take Mike and Annabelle to the reception—a vintage Rolls Royce that Ted had restored. It had been his pet project for the past ten years, and Annabelle was to be his first passenger. Philippa had wondered about the wisdom of this, but Annabelle had had no such qualms. "We will be honoured, Ted!" she had said when he offered. This had provided Ted with the impetus to complete the project, and he had marvelled how he had been able to get more done in the past month than he had in the previous nine years. He could finally justify the immense cost and time he had poured into the classic vehicle.

Next, Annabelle and Philippa visited the bridesmaids to give them their instructions and bring them their dresses. Bonnie and her friend Felicity were simply beside themselves with excitement. They could not stop bursting into fits of giggles.

Looking on indulgently, broad smiles spread over their faces, were Annabelle's brother Roger, and her parents,

Petronella and Raymond. Her parents had arrived in Upton St. Mary the evening before. Raymond was a black cab driver in London, and there had been some speculation that it would be his car that would take Annabelle to the reception and not Ted's. After much agonising, Raymond Dixon had plucked up the courage to phone Annabelle and tell her he would leave the cab at home. He was too nervous about his speech to drive.

"Hi Mum, hi Dad, hi Roger," Annabelle said, giving them each a peck.

"All set?" Roger said, grinning. He'd waited a long time for this day.

"Not really." Annabelle pulled a face. "But I'm getting there. You?"

"Smashing," he said, rocking on his heels.

"I've got my outfit and my hat," Mrs. Dixon said, pointing to a suit carrier hanging off a wardrobe in the corner and a large hat box on the floor.

"You're going to look fabulous, Mum. Dad?"

Raymond Dixon pulled at his collar. He looked a bit pale. "I'm sure I'll be fine, love."

"I've got to rush off now, but I'll see you at the rehearsal tonight. Supper at the cottage afterwards, okay?"

Everyone nodded, the girls giggled, and Annabelle and Philippa left to pick up Mrs. Shoreditch, Mary, and Harper, cramming them all into Annabelle's small car. Mary got the front passenger seat—a kindness to the others.

Annabelle whizzed them back to the cottage, where the heated, passionate matter of last-minute adjustments to Annabelle's dress began. Annabelle had chosen a white silk dress with lace to the base of her neck and down to her wrists. She had been unsure about the full skirt, worried she might trip, but Philippa had persuaded her that it was more modest.

"I can take in the waist a little more," said Mrs. Shoreditch.

"I can barely breathe as it is!" replied Annabelle.

"Have you considered a corset?" Mrs. Shoreditch asked.

"Are you sure that's appropriate?" Mary wondered.

"That train is an accident waiting to happen," Philippa said.

"Oh, stop! It's wonderful!" Harper cried.

"You know how clumsy Annabelle is, and with a corset, she'll be oxygen deprived!" Philippa countered.

"Philippa!" That was Annabelle.

After much back-and-forth, the women reached a consensus. Mrs. Shoreditch hurried away to carry out the alterations they had settled upon. It was now late into the afternoon, the sun already setting behind the church.

But there was still more to do. A call to Sophie and Gabriella confirmed they were expecting the wedding party and guests around noon the next day, the wine from Ville d'Eauloise had arrived, a generator was available so that Mr. Trilby's ice cream didn't melt, and there was sufficient clotted cream for the scones and the hedgehogs. The balloon animal man and face painter for the children was confirmed, the photographer agreed to come to the cottage before the wedding and stay throughout the reception, and the Cornish pasty man was working well into the night making several hundred beef and potato pasties. When Annabelle rushed off to the wedding rehearsal, Philippa prepared a light supper for twenty.

Later that night after everyone had left, Annabelle and Philippa stood at the kitchen window watching the stars in the night sky whilst enjoying a much-needed cup of tea. Everything was ready.

"How're you feeling, Philippa?"

"Shouldn't I be asking you that?"

"I'm tired, but happy."

"Me too."

Annabelle frowned. "Is that clock broken?"

Philippa looked at the antique clock which sat on the stand in the hallway. "No," she said, fatigue seeping into her voice. "It's eleven o'clock. You're twelve hours away from being a married woman."

"I feel as if I need sixteen hours of sleep," Annabelle quipped.

Philippa flicked through the notepad which had been her constant companion during the day. "Hmm," she said as she frowned at the pages. "I think we're about done. We'll still have a few hours tomorrow morning if anything pops up— though I imagine you'll be too nervous to do anything."

"Actually, I'm not nervous at all. I'm excited!" Annabelle said, smiling warmly. "As long as Mike shows up, I'll be fine. He better not run off!"

Philippa's face morphed into an expression of horror.

"Oh, calm down, Philippa!" Annabelle chuckled. "It was just a joke."

"I wouldn't joke about such things, Reverend. How did the rehearsal go?"

"Fine," Annabelle said. "My dad can hardly tell one end of the aisle from another he's so nervous and the girls can barely stand up straight for laughing, but it went well. Although it'll be weird taking instructions from someone else in my own church."

"A nice weird though," Philippa said, smiling. She put her cup and saucer by the sink and tied her apron around her.

"Here, I can wash up," Annabelle said. "And again, thank you. I can't express how much gratitude I have for you doing all of this whilst I was . . . well, busy. I don't deserve you."

Philippa smiled as she put on her coat. "Reverend, seeing you married to a lovely, handsome, respectable man is all the thanks I need."

Annabelle beamed as she put on her own apron. She was pretty relieved too.

CHAPTER FORTY-FOUR

QUIET EXCITEMENT CREPT across the village of Upton St. Mary as the first beams of a bright, spring sun pierced a clear sky. Alarms peeped, trilled, and jingled, waking people to the momentous day. Parents ordered children out of bed with little sympathy. Shirts were ironed, dresses were inspected, and texts were sent as people arranged and confirmed timings and travel plans. The sun shone now, but the British weather being what it was, there was no guarantee there would be any sign of it in a few hours. The villagers repeatedly checked for clouds as those who would later picnic on the lawn outside the reception marquee gathered their rugs, deckchairs, and umbrellas.

With four hours to go, a team of florists, their arms full of blooms, quietly let themselves into the church. At Flynn's, Katie had been up for hours. At No. 10 Market Street, 101-year-old Mrs. Polightly was dressed and sitting in her favourite chair, patiently waiting. She was ready. Nothing would make her late for this wedding, and at her age, four hours was nothing. There was always tea, many cups of tea, to pass the time.

Harper Jones was awoken by the alarm on her phone, and after rolling to turn it off, she rolled in the other direction to wake her husband. She found his side of the bed empty. The pathologist sat up in bed and looked about the small room of Mrs. Sutton's bed and breakfast.

"Nick?" she called out curiously. "Are you in the bathroom?" She waited for a moment. When there was no answer, she quickly tossed off the covers and got out of bed. "Nick?" she called out again, a little more anxious now. The bathroom was empty.

Beyond her bedroom door, she heard rumblings of movement, footsteps, the occasional low voice. Harper threw a hoodie over her pyjamas, slid into some shoes, and tentatively opened the door to inspect the passage. "Nick!" she cried as she saw her husband dressed in Lycra, guiding his expensive, carbon-framed bike through the passage. "What on earth are you doing?"

"I'm just heading out for a quick ride. It's a gorgeous day."

"We've got a wedding to go to!" she exclaimed.

"I know," Nick conceded, glancing quickly at his watch. "But we've got ages 'til it starts. That's loads of time. I'll ride for a couple of hours, get back, quick shower, then off we go!"

Harper shook her head, astonished that this was happening. "And what if you get lost?"

"How could I get lost?" Nick said, tapping the phone attached to his handlebars. "GPS. Look, you know how I get when I've not had my ride. And we've been to three weddings in the past year and not one started on time, did they?" Harper gazed at him, too sleepy and too surprised to come up with a response.

"Morning! There's fresh coffee if you'd like some," Mrs. Sutton called from the end of the passage.

"There you go," Nick said, wheeling his bike forwards. "Have a cup of coffee and I'll be back before you know it." He leant over his bike and kissed his wife quickly. He called back over his shoulder, "See you in a bit, darling."

Harper was just about to yell a final, parting retort—something about men—before Mrs. Sutton stepped into her view. Mrs. Sutton had been running her B and B for thirty years and was justifiably proud of her reputation for offering "the most amazing breakfasts in the West Country," as afforded her by TourGuide, the online review site. "Coffee, Doctor Jones? Tea? Would you like me to bring it to your room? I can also cook you a full English. It'll keep your strength up for the day. Those photos can take such a long time, can't they? Or there's fresh fruit, toast and marmalade, cereal, or eggs if you want something smaller. Best to eat now, eh? It'll be an exciting but long day, no doubt."

"Um," Harper started. "Yes, okay. I could do with some coffee actually." She checked herself in the hall mirror and decided she looked passable, then walked to the dining room where Samuel Bellingham and Father John were chatting over breakfast.

CHAPTER FORTY-FIVE

"MORNING, HARPER," FATHER John said as he stood up. "Ready for the big day?" He peered over her shoulder. "Er, I just saw your husband leaving."

"Yes," Harper said as she took a seat at the table beside Bellingham. "He's decided that now is the perfect time to gallivant around the Cornish countryside. But what are you doing here?"

"Oh, Katie is too busy preparing for the wedding, so she sent all her guests down here for breakfast. Everyone's pulling together, aren't they? I love to see it."

"How did the rehearsal go last night?"

"Fine, fine. Pretty standard for a rehearsal. Lots of nervous giggling. Mr. Dixon was as white as a sheet, poor man. I think he'll be very happy when this evening comes around." Father John checked his watch. "If you don't mind, I must take my leave of you. I'm going to go for a short walk over to Annabelle's. Check on the bride, you know, make sure she won't do a runner, and then over to the church to run through everything for a final time—stage, sound, that kind of thing. Wouldn't want to let Annabelle down today of all days. See you later, Harper. Nice to have met you, Bellingham. Good luck on the rest of your journey." Samuel Bellingham stood with Father John. The two men shook hands.

"Bye, Father. Good luck!" Harper said warmly.

When he had left, Samuel Bellingham spoke. "Can I get you some coffee, Harper?"

"That would be lovely." Harper shook her head at the offer of sugar. "I didn't expect you to still be here today," she said. "How's the leg holding up?"

"Much better," Bellingham said, extending it as proof. "I'll be off later. Continuing my little ramble across Cornwall."

"Very good." Harper smiled as she sipped her coffee.

"And how are you?"

"I'm looking forward to today. It's been a long time coming. I don't think it will be just the father of the bride who will sleep more soundly tonight."

"It all sounds quite the to-do."

"Annabelle is much loved in the village. They can hardly wait to see her happily married."

"You don't live here, do you?"

"No, I live on the other side of Truro. I'm the local pathologist, so I cover this area. It just so happens that the murder victim at the farm was my aunt."

"Will you be leaving after the wedding?"

Harper put her coffee cup down and stretched a little. "No. I'll stay on to help my other aunt and sort out a few things. I'm inheriting the farm. There's a lot to do."

"I see." Bellingham frowned. "Your aunt isn't the beneficiary?" He quickly glanced at Harper. "Forgive me. Village gossip . . ."

Harper grabbed a fresh slice of toast from the replenished rack Mrs. Sutton had put on the table. She began to spread marmalade on it. "No, Aunt Joan was adopted and always understood that the farm would pass to Aunt Kathleen's brother, my father, on Aunt Kathleen's death. He died two years ago, so the farm comes to me. Not my doing, but the farm has been in our family for generations. It was all set up this way long ago."

"So, you and your Aunt Kathleen were blood relations?"

"Yes." Harper assessed Bellingham. His line of questioning was getting . . . strange.

Bellingham smiled at her. "It's just that I heard that your aunt was adopted, and that you and she were . . . well, very similar. That you look so alike. I assumed you were related to her, not Kathleen."

Harper laughed and took a bite of toast. "Yes," she said. "Very common mistake. I look just like Aunt Joan; I'm often mistaken for her daughter. But we're not related in that sense. I love her just the same though. I never cared to make a distinction between her or Kathleen."

"I see," Bellingham said, his features clouded now, a faraway look in his eyes.

They sat for a while, sipping their drinks, munching on toast, and exchanging small talk regarding the village, the wedding, and the stalling of the murder case. Eventually, Bellingham checked his watch. "Do you have time to go for a walk, perhaps?"

"A walk?" Harper said.

"Yes," Bellingham replied, suddenly a little bashful. "I thought testing the old leg would be a good idea before I leave. One last stroll around these lovely surroundings before I find greener pastures. I mean, I'm sure you have plenty of other things to do this morning, but I'd love some company, and it's still a while until the wedding."

"Hmm," Harper said, checking her watch and considering the time.

"Fifteen minutes, tops," he said, smiling.

Harper looked at the man's cheerful face, then around her at the breakfasting guests. "Why not? If my husband has enough time to romp around this morning, then why don't I? Let me get my jacket."

"That's the spirit." Bellingham laughed. He watched Harper as she walked off to get her things. Through the window of the swing door to the kitchen, Mrs. Sutton was peering, monitoring the status of her guests' breakfasts. As Harper walked away, she noticed Samuel Bellingham's smile slowly disappear. It was replaced with a nasty sneer before he left to go to his room.

CHAPTER FORTY-SIX

"STAND STILL, ANNABELLE! I can't do these buttons up!"

"Oof. I can barely breathe!"

"Stop breathing then! And stop running about, Dougie! You nearly trod on Annabelle's train!"

"Go outside and play with Bonnie and Felicity, Dougie. I know they're girls, but you can manage it for one day."

"Noooo! The dogs will join them! Five minutes and they'll all be covered in mud!"

The inside of Annabelle's cottage was filled with a storm of pink dresses, bouquets, rampaging children, and fluttering bridesmaids. The scents of fresh blooms and perfume permeated the air as the women chattered and bustled about the living room where Annabelle stood in her dress.

"Philippa," Mary called from the kitchen, "do you happen to know where the video camera is?"

"Video camera?" Philippa said as she fought with the back of Annabelle's dress. "It's on the kitchen counter—if one of the children hasn't pinched it! Use your phone if you can't find it."

Barbara from the Dog and Duck knocked on the front door and let herself in. This was no time to stand on formalities. "We've not got enough glasses!" she said, resplendent in a vibrant violet suit with matching hat and lipstick. "The wine and champagne are all set up in the reception tent, but all we have are beer glasses to drink it from!"

Still grappling with the twenty or so silk-covered buttons on the back of Annabelle's dress, Philippa said, "Sophie and Gabriella ordered lots of wine glasses and champagne flutes from the party supplies company. They're probably inside the big house. Just ask Sophie or Gabriella to get them for you."

"But Sophie and Gabriella are here!" Barbara said, pointing at the two women who were trying on shoes in the hallway.

With an extra push, Philippa managed to slip the loop over the final button. She stood back, panting. As she considered how Annabelle looked, Philippa said, "Ask the gardener, Albert Roper, then. He'll know where they are. And he'll have a key."

"Right," Barbara said, scurrying away with her phone to her ear.

"Breathe in," Philippa ordered.

Annabelle did as she was told. It seemed the best thing to do in the circumstances. She inhaled slowly, holding her breath at the top before exhaling equally as slowly, just like she'd observed during the natural childbirth classes held in the church hall. When nothing burst, she tried again, a little more quickly and deeply. Still good.

She gazed at herself in the mirror as Philippa came to her side and looked at her reflection. Her ivory dress shimmered in the light. Lace covered her arms and shoulders and continued over a silk bodice that nipped in at Annabelle's waist before flowing over a full-panelled skirt and finishing in a small train that streamed behind her. "Oh!" Annabelle said. She was enchanted. She barely recognised herself. "What do you think, Philippa?"

Philippa was lost for words. It was as though the sight of Annabelle in her wedding dress was the culmination of her entire life's work. Which, in a way, it was.

"Philippa," Samira Malik called suddenly, clutching a phone to her ear. The daughter of the couple who ran the village shop had come home from university specially to attend the wedding. "Do you have the seating plan for the reception? Aziz says he can't put the name cards out without it."

At that moment, Mary zoomed in with her phone. She videoed the scene of Annabelle in her dress admiring herself in front of the mirror. She held the phone well out in front of her to avoid getting her bump in the picture. "How on earth did we hold weddings before there were phones, Annabelle?"

Mary paused for Annabelle's reply, but Annabelle was distracted. She was looking in the full-length mirror, her attention captured by the reflection of Philippa's face turning a ghostly white, her eyes widening until they were two round, black discs, like tunnels to her soul.

CHAPTER FORTY-SEVEN

"PHILIPPA?" ANNABELLE SAID.
"Philippa?" Samira repeated.
The room went quiet; everyone frozen in place. Even the children stopped playing their games as they sensed the sudden chill that filled the air. All eyes were on Philippa as she gawped into the middle distance. Suddenly she spun to face the room, revealing her terrified expression to everyone around her. "The seating plan . . . I forgot to review the seating plan."

There was a second of confusion as the women processed the meaning of her words, followed by pandemonium as Philippa pressed every woman into action. They began clambering over and bumping into each other as they sought to find the missing seating plan with an urgency normally only reserved for a national emergency, the type when they bring in the army.

"'It was on a big sheet!'" Philippa called out above the chaos of fancy dresses and flowers. "Look for a big sheet of paper!"

"Could this be it?" Mary said, waving her hand by her

knees as she attempted, and failed, to bend over to pick up a large, rolled-up sheet of paper from behind the sofa.

"Hurrah!" Philippa called. "Bring it over here."

Once Biscuit had been unceremoniously dumped off the table with a mewling protest, along with a few of Annabelle's favourite ornaments, Philippa spread out the seating plan. The women gathered in a circle around it.

"Someone, get us a pen!" Philippa called.

"Pen coming up!" called Bonnie as she paused her giggling and went to her box of coloured felt-tips.

"What's this?" Samira said as she looked at the names scrawled on the map. "You've got my parents sitting apart!"

"It was just a first draft!" Philippa cried. "I planned to go through it with Annabelle yesterday, but I forgot in the rush for the cakes, the flowers, the dress, and all the other one hundred and one things we had to do!"

"You've put Mrs. Brinsmead next to Mrs. Swift!" exclaimed Barbara. "You know what they're like. They'll talk all through the speeches!"

"No, they won't. You're exaggerating, Barbara," someone said.

"I am not! Those two talk during funerals. A wedding would be no problem!"

"Move Mr. Prudden nearer the exit. He's got a bladder the size of a pea."

"Mrs. Royce should be as far from Mrs. Seymour as possible. They had a terrible argument over dog poop last week."

With a seriousness that came with the knowledge that hers was a very important role, Bonnie poked a pen into the huddle. Philippa took it, hurriedly crossing out and rewriting names according to the suggestions thrown her way.

"There are too many men on that table. It'll get rowdy. It needs a few women to keep the noise down."

"Mrs. Biddlecombe is too far from the top table. She's terribly sensitive about that sort of thing. We'll never hear the end of it."

"Samira," Philippa said as she scribbled on the map. "Do you mind not sitting with your parents?"

"No," the girl said. "Maybe you could sit me next to Ryan?"

The room went silent. "He's an old friend," Samira added, her eyes widening innocently. There was a pause, then the frenzy resumed.

"Don't put Dr. Horsham too close to the bar."

"Move that ladies' man, Mr. Beardsley. Putting him next to a pretty young girl like Zara is an incident waiting to happen."

"Could you move Mrs. Curtis from my table? I like the woman, but I'd also like to have my fair share of the food."

"Stop!" Annabelle shouted. She'd been listening silently, allowing the women to have their say, but now she peered at the map, leaning down to see it a little closer before putting her finger on a name. "Who is this?"

Philippa leant in to read it. "Simon Butterworth," she said, looking up at the ring of faces around the table. "Anyone know him?"

The women looked at each other. They shook their heads, exchanged shrugs, and pursed lips.

"Why is this name here?" Annabelle asked Philippa. "Who is he?"

Philippa shrugged. "I don't know," she answered before pulling out her notebook and flicking through it. "Here it is. His name is grouped with Harper and her husband. Yes, I got this from Mrs. Sutton's bed and breakfast. It's a list of people staying there. I presumed every one of them was here for the wedding. If no one knows who Simon Butterworth is, then I suppose he's just a random B and B guest and nothing to do with it." Philippa crossed out the name. "Not a problem. More space at the table."

"Oh, but it's a problem alright!" Annabelle said, picking up her skirt and marching around the women to her front door. "It's very much a problem indeed!"

CHAPTER FORTY-EIGHT

"YOUR PEDICURE ISN'T dry!" cried Sophie.
"Flip-flops!" finished Gabriella.
"Where are you going?" cried Mary.

But Annabelle was already out of the cottage, clutching her bunched-up dress about her as she opened the door to her Mini.

"No!" shouted Philippa. "Not the Mini! You'll ruin your dress!"

"I'm sorry!" Annabelle said. "But I have to do this!" Within seconds, Annabelle had revved the engine and reversed the Mini out of its parking spot. She aimed it forwards, targeting the open gate.

"Not without me you won't!" Philippa said. Running alongside the moving car, she quickly opened the passenger-side door and jumped in.

"What's going on?" Barbara asked the cluster of women who gathered at the door watching as the Mini sped away from the church.

"I told you she had cold feet!"
"We can't just let her run away like this!"

"She needs a good talking to—oh!"

The women were roughly shoved aside, and Mary appeared in the doorway, holding her flowers. "To the cars!" she cried, raising her bouquet like a torch, or maybe a sword.

With the knack that heavily pregnant women have for getting what they want, on Mary's command the women rushed to their cars. Within seconds, they too were leaving deep ruts in the courtyard gravel as they sped off in pursuit of the bride's Mini Cooper.

Inside the Mini, Philippa shrieked, "What are you doing, Annabelle?" She cried out again as she clutched the dashboard and braced herself against the door in the rolling, swinging car.

"Butterworth!" Annabelle said as she leant over her steering wheel, gripping it so hard her knuckles were as white as her dress.

"What?"

"That was the name of the witch-hunter in Martha George's diary!"

"So?" Philippa cried, still utterly bewildered.

"Unusual name, don't you think? Never heard it around these parts before, have you? No, I didn't think so. This is the best clue yet as to the identity of Kathleen Webster's killer! Maybe this Butterworth fellow is the murderer!"

When Annabelle arrived at the B&B, Mrs. Sutton was finishing breakfast. Screeching tires outside caught her attention. She peered anxiously out of the window. Confusion and surprise quickly changed to amazement when the door to the bed and breakfast burst open and Annabelle, in full wedding regalia, the skirt of her dress in one hand and clutching her tiara and veil to her head with the other, strode in. She was quickly followed by a crowd of flower-clutching bridesmaids and large-hatted women.

Annabelle marched up to Mrs. Sutton's tiny check-in counter and pinged the bell as the women gathered around her, some of them attempting to snatch up Annabelle's train to keep it from dragging on the floor. Mrs. Sutton stared, speechless and stunned and a little afraid.

"Hello, Mrs. Sutton," Annabelle said officiously.

"H-hello? Is there something the matter? Something I can do for you? Is there a problem with the wedding I can help with?" Mrs. Sutton looked anxiously at the doorway to her dining room, through which the heads of curious guests poked.

"I have something very important to ask you. It's a matter of extreme urgency and deep significance."

"Yes, of course," Mrs. Sutton said, growing visibly stressed now. She stood to attention and stared straight ahead, willing to do whatever was asked of her as all good bride's attendants do. "Whatever you need. You are the bride, and it is your wedding day."

"Have you a man called Butterworth staying here?"

Mrs. Sutton twisted her head to look at Annabelle. She frowned. "What?" She hesitated, but seeing the thrust of Annabelle's jaw, she quickly resumed her military stance and looked straight ahead again. "Butterworth? No . . . That name doesn't ring a bell."

"We must leave, Reverend," Philippa pleaded at her side. "We've still got your makeup to do!"

Ignoring her, Annabelle continued, "You gave Philippa a list of guests, and on that list was a man named Simon Butterworth. Do you remember?"

"Hmm," Mrs. Sutton said, looking at her computer.

"Let me see. The list I gave Philippa was simply a printout of our bookings." The woman tapped expertly on her keyboard for a few seconds as Annabelle leant over the counter in suspense. "Ah! Here it is. Yes, we do have someone who used a credit card with that name."

"So, he was here?"

Mrs. Sutton traced a finger across her computer screen. "Well, that was the name on the credit card, but the actual booking was made under the name of Samuel Bellingham."

Annabelle's jaw dropped. Her face turned as white as her dress. "Samuel Bellingham?"

Mrs. Sutton nodded. "Yes."

"And where is he now?"

"Oh . . . He went out with Harper an hour or so ago."

"Nooooooooo!" Annabelle shouted, slamming a palm on the counter, startling everyone. "I've got to find him! Where did he go?"

Shaken by the vicar's manner, Mrs. Sutton replied, "I-I think they went for a walk across the fields," she said, pointing behind her to indicate the land beyond the bed and breakfast. "To the woods by the travellers' camp."

Annabelle nodded her thanks to Mrs. Sutton. She spun around quickly, her flip-flops squeaking on the hardwood floor, and marched to the door. The bridesmaids and large-hatted women quickly moved out of her way before closing in behind her, still clutching her train as they excitedly followed.

CHAPTER FORTY-NINE

MIKE LOOKED AT his watch. An hour to go. He wanted to be there in plenty of time.

His sister, Chantelle, was his best woman. His unusual choice had thrilled and surprised Annabelle, who'd expected him to go for one of his police mates from way back, but Mike was close to his sister, and he couldn't think of anyone better suited for the job. Chantelle was a master baker and had spent the early part of the morning helping Katie Flynn finish the sweets for the wedding, then he and Chantelle had spent an hour going over their speeches before it was time to get gussied up.

Mike had grown rather fond of dressing smartly since he got together with Annabelle. He took seriously his role as the future husband of a beloved village vicar and figured he could not be seen as a casual, slovenly wretch. It would reflect badly on his bride. He enjoyed the way well-fitted suits and shiny, elegant shoes compelled him to pin his shoulders back, raise his head, and draw himself up to his full height. He enjoyed the change from his typical workmanlike trench coat and boots. Most of all, however, he appreciated the particular glint of attraction in Annabelle's eyes whenever she saw him in stylish attire.

His mind cast back to that irritating, but well-dressed French inspector, Babineaux, with whom he'd worked on a case and who had given him some good advice on love. The Frenchman had made an impression. Mike had even been working out at the gym. He'd wanted to lose a few pounds that he blamed Philippa's cooking for.

His appearance was merely one of many reasons Mike arrived at the church feeling proud, content, and excited. He walked through the arched stone entrance, the outside of which was now decorated with a huge garland of pink roses offset by purple hydrangeas, white lily of the valley, and a flurry of green foliage. Standing in the entry porch, he peeked into the ancient church. Inside, he could see more flowers, white ribbons, and the primary school choir setting up for their performance. Satisfied, he went to stand in the sunshine to exchange smiles and small talk, and accept the well-wishes of arriving guests.

"Nearly time for liftoff, Mike," Roger, Annabelle's brother and one of the ushers, hissed in his ear. The pair had become friendly in the months since they first met on the Scottish island of Blodraigh where Roger lived.

Mike checked the time and cast another smile across the church pews as people streamed in from outside and found their seats. "Yep," he said.

Chantelle, standing by his side in a lavender trouser suit, put her arm though his. "Come on, bruv. Let's do this." As Mike and Chantelle walked into the church, Father John saw them and smiled. Everything was going like clockwork. He looked around. The church was packed. It was standing room only, and with the whole village invited, the congregation had spilt outside. They would watch the ceremony on their phones via a live feed set up by Tony Pritchard, the local IT technician and sometime DJ who lived in the village but who hadn't been in a church since his christening twenty years before. Everyone was a little restless. Father John put it down to excitement.

Mike was engaged in conversation with the priest when Constable Derbyshire ran into the church. Beads of sweat dribbled down the constable's forehead, the whites of his eyes clearly visible even at a distance. Slowing his pace, Derbyshire sidled up the aisle. "Sir," he whispered loudly. "Sir, sir!" He frantically beckoned the inspector to him whilst trying desperately to be inconspicuous. He was a uniformed police officer scurrying furtively up the centre aisle of a church full of wedding guests a few minutes before the ceremony was due to start. Inconspicuous he was not.

Mike looked on with incomprehension as the young officer bent double to gather his breath. "What's wrong, Derbyshire?"

The young policeman straightened, looked around him, then leant in, compelling both Father John and Mike to do the same. "Annabelle. No, I mean Mrs. Dixon. Wait, Mrs. Mike. Or Reverend. Sorry."

"Reverend is fine," Father John offered helpfully.

"Thank you, sir," Derbyshire gasped, still panting for air. His eyes widened. "She's gone!"

Mike waited for a few seconds, sure that more words would come. When it became clear that they wouldn't and that the constable was awaiting a response, he said, "Gone? What do you mean, gone?"

"I just saw her running away across the Websters' land towards the travellers' camp. A lot of the womenfolk are with her, sir. They seemed to be trying to stop her, but she's hoofing it. She's galloping like a horse, sir."

"When was this?"

Derbyshire looked at his watch. "About five minutes ago."

Something stabbed at the core of Mike's being, fixing him in place. His blood ran cold. Old Jonquil's face swam into his mind, and once again he felt dizzy like he had in her small caravan at the camp.

Seeing him sway, Father John discreetly reached out to steady the inspector. "I'm sure there's a perfectly good explanation, Mike," the priest assured him quietly, hoping no one in the church had noticed the sickly green hue that had spread across Mike's face.

"Explanation or not, she can't marry me if she's not here," Mike whispered.

"Derbyshire," Father John said with all the authority the inspector usually claimed for himself but was quite unable to bring forth at this moment. "Find another officer and a police car and get after Annabelle. Find out what's going on." Derbyshire nodded vigorously, glad to be told what to do.

Father John turned to Mike. "Come with me to the church office. We don't want you fainting in front of a crowd."

"Why would she run away?" Mike said in a small voice. "I don't understand."

Father John sighed as he guided the inspector to the back of the church. "I don't think you're supposed to understand, Mike. Welcome to marriage."

CHAPTER FIFTY

"WHAT ARE YOU doing? It's eleven a.m.! I'm supposed to be at Annabelle's wedding. Let me go!"

Simon Butterworth had clutched Harper by the arm and dragged her along behind him as soon as she realised they were not going for a fifteen-minute stroll.

"Where are you taking me?" Harper struggled, but the man was holding her tight.

"Shut up, woman." All the geniality he'd radiated earlier had left Butterworth, as had his limp. "You think I'm going to let you go?"

"What do you want with me? I haven't done anything to you." Harper continued to push and shove the man, determined to make whatever he was planning to do with her as difficult as possible. They were at the bottom of a long, steep hill. They were both panting. She gave him one hard shove with her shoulder. He twisted around to face her, his eyes wild. He grabbed her by both arms and gave her a shake.

"Stop struggling and submit to your fate! I am Simon

Butterworth, great-great-great grandson of the famed witch-hunter Edward Butterworth!"

Harper refused to be cowed. "And?"

"And you are a witch!"

"What?" Harper gaped at him. She stopped struggling. "Are you mad?"

"You and your aunt are descendants of Martha George, a witch who used her evil powers to evade capture by my ancestor. Did you not know that witches beget more witches? All female offspring are deemed of the same class. They must be expunged. It is my destiny to eradicate them. I am avenging my ancestor's soul!"

"You killed my aunt? Because of some medieval conspiracy theory?"

"It wasn't difficult. The pitchfork was very convenient."

"Wha—Did you steal the notebook too?"

"Yes, that foolish old man thought I was his friend. Pah! He's a traitor to his kind. The church has lost its way and harbours, even supports evil women like you. They know not of what they are dealing with."

"You are out of your mind!" Harper struggled again, but she could feel herself tiring as they began to climb the steep hill.

Butterworth shook his fist in the air. "Your aunt was without issue, and I believed she was the end of the line, that my job was done. I thought my great-great-great grandfather's soul could now rest in peace. But then I found you!"

"Eh?"

"I tracked your great-great-great grandmother here. It wasn't difficult. I have papers, journals, sermons—all recorded by the great man, Butterworth. The historical marriage record and the name Webster gave me more clues. Martha George, a widow, married Conor Webster of Webster's Farm. Kathleen Webster lived at Webster's Farm. It didn't take a genius to work out she and Martha were related. But I overlooked you. Stupid gossips! They have their uses, especially when it comes to outing witches, but they are notoriously inaccurate and I made the mistake of not checking carefully enough. When I asked around, my inquiries led me to believe you were related to the other aunt, the one I learnt was adopted. One woman even thought you were her daughter. Pah! But now I know better, I will do better."

"You're being ridiculous. Let me go. I have a wedding to attend!" Harper attempted to shake Butterworth off, but he clung tight.

"It is you who are being ridiculous. Your fate is sealed. There's no going back now."

"There they are!" shouted Philippa.

"Where?"

"There! Almost at the bottom of that hill! Harper and that chap!"

The sight of her prey drove Annabelle on. With a spurt of energy, her flip-flops squelched in the mud, the women around her struggling to keep up.

"Ooh! Slow down! I almost stepped in something!"

"I don't know if I can go on much longer!"

"This is terribly exciting! Much better than the last wedding I went to!"

After a final sprint, the figures were close enough to be unmistakable. Samuel Bellingham and Harper Jones trudged their way up the hill which marked the end of the

Webster sisters' land. Bellingham seemed to have Harper by the wrist as he led the way.

"Stop!" cried Annabelle with the last of her breath as she slowed down within fifty feet of them.

With her shout, the two figures ahead of her spun around. Annabelle and her motley maids were a sight to behold. Annabelle stood in front, an expression of fear on her face, her tiara askew atop her disheveled hairdo. There was a large mud stain down her dress. Mary, pink-cheeked and defiant at Annabelle's shoulder, held her bump protectively. Around them were a gaggle of red-faced women and young girls of various shapes and sizes, many of them wearing large hats, all of them out of breath, and several still clutching at the train of the wedding dress as though they might roll back down the hill if they let go.

"Annabelle!" Harper shouted, unsure whether to laugh or be afraid. "Be careful! This man is a madman!"

"Get away from him!" Annabelle shouted as she clambered closer, reluctantly followed by her posse. "He's the one who killed your aunt!"

"He confessed!" Harper cried. She turned to look at her companion, the husky, dark-haired man in country tweeds. He looked back at her innocently.

"Unhand her, you beast!" Annabelle cried.

Harper felt an arm tighten around her chest, pinning her arms to her sides. A sensation of cold metal pressing against her neck forced her to twist backwards. Bellingham had pulled out a musket. He held it against the pathologist, his face morphing into a manic mask of malevolence. The women around Annabelle shrieked.

"Get back!" Bellingham shouted, his voice bouncing around the valley. "Get back or I kill her right in front of you!"

"What are you doing?" Harper managed to say from her precarious position.

"What is this? Some kind of historical vengeance?" shouted Annabelle.

Butterworth growled. "That's exactly what it is. Witches are a scourge. They and their blood relatives must be extinguished!" he shouted.

"But why?" Annabelle asked, throwing her hand up in exasperation.

"Why? You ask why? I perform an act that my family has carried out for generations: the eradication of witches. I destroy an evil passed down the bloodline and unimaginable to mortals. I fulfil my destiny. And you ask me why? Two centuries ago, you pathetic, simple-minded morons would have revered me. You would have celebrated and followed and helped me destroy these . . . these . . ."—he looked at Harper, a diabolical sneer spreading across his face as he gritted his teeth—"demons. But now look at you; all you do is hinder! You've become agents of evil with your passivity. Content to sit by whilst witches roam amongst you. There's a battle between good and evil raging amongst us, and you are blind to it!"

Annabelle stepped forwards carefully. "You've already killed Kathleen," she said calmly. "Harper has nothing to do with this. Let her go."

CHAPTER FIFTY-ONE

BUTTERWORTH SNARLED AND then laughed vengefully. "A typical trick," he said. His mouth twisted into a vicious grin. "Appealing to my conscience. You do not understand. She is of the same bloodline. This woman possesses as much evil as those already dispatched." Butterworth tightened his grip on Harper.

"Stop this!" Philippa cried.

"Are you ready?" Butterworth whispered into Harper's ear, pressing the barrel of the antique gun harder into her neck. "It may look old, but this is a working firearm, and I am ready to use it."

It was evident to the women they were seconds away from witnessing a murder, their shrieks and cries useless in the presence of this crazed lunatic. Some of them covered their eyes, others turned away, most of them continued to scream. Only Annabelle stood firm, quiet, and determined. She raised her chin. "You will do no such thing. With the power vested in me by the Lord, I command you unhand this woman who is no more a witch than I."

Butterworth laughed a dirty, contemptuous, monstrous laugh. "You think your words mean anything to m—"

The muscular, gleaming black horse bore down on Butterworth, his hooves thundering down the hill as he carried a man on his back almost as large as he. For a split second, the pair was outlined against the clear blue sky; the next they were at the gun-wielding witch-hunter's shoulder at a gallop.

"Yah!" Dylan, the travelling bear-man bellowed from atop his horse as he kicked out at the figures standing just below. The kick sent Butterworth and Harper flying in opposite directions. Harper tumbled towards the women, who immediately surrounded her, acting as a protective shroud, their large hats bumping as they bent over to care for her. Butterworth splayed on the ground, quickly scrabbling to his feet as he sought to escape. Dylan sharply brought his horse around, once again charging the man on the ground but stopping just as he expected to be trampled. The horse reared on its hind legs, a mountain of muscle and sinew. Butterworth put his arm up. "Argh!" The horse snorted heavily and pawed at the ground with its large, tough, hairy hooves only a foot or so from Butterworth's head. It was enough to prevent the killer from getting to his feet.

At Annabelle's shoulder, Mary whispered. "Annabelle, look! It's the Cornovii!"

Annabelle watched the scene unfold in front of her, shielding her eyes from the penetrating rays of the midday sun. Her gaze was drawn to the highest point of the hill, where flashes of light attracted her attention. The travellers, marching in a broad line across the hill's ridge, emerged over the crest. Each of them brandished a weapon. Lengths of piping and heavy chains glinted in the sun. Even the children wielded wooden sticks.

"No, Mary, that's not the Cornovii. They're the travellers."

With little fuss and in almost complete silence, the travellers marched down the hill as one, a modern-day tribe ready for trouble and prepared to deal with it. They were a formidable sight. When they reached Butterworth, they quietly tied the killer's hands behind his back and lifted him to his feet as Dylan sought to keep his excited, prancing horse under control a few feet away.

Annabelle walked over to him. "Thank you!" Annabelle said. "How did you . . .? Why did . . .?"

Dylan laughed gently. "Jonquil said something was going on beyond the hill, something serious. We tooled up and came to take a look."

Annabelle considered this for a moment. "How did she know? Did she see it in a vision? Sense it?"

Dylan laughed more heartily now. He dismounted and gave his horse a brisk pat. "No. She heard it. Pretty difficult not to considering twenty women were screaming like banshees a few yards from her caravan."

Annabelle sighed, then laughed with relief alongside the huge bearish man, only stopping when they heard sirens approaching.

"We'll be off then," Dylan said, his voice tinged with regret when he saw the police cars.

"Thank you," Annabelle said. "I won't forget this."

"I believe you," Dylan said. "But most people will. They always do."

"They won't," Annabelle insisted.

Annabelle walked back to the women, who were still huddling together. Harper was standing against a tree, apparently unharmed by her ordeal. Annabelle checked on her. "How are you?"

"I'm fine." Harper took a deep breath. "We need to get you married though. Can't hang around here. Come on, ladies, let's go!" she called out, as practical and no-nonsense as ever.

"We can't leave," one of the women with an extremely large, red hat said.

"Why-ever not?"

"It's Mary. She's in labour."

Annabelle's eyes widened. "Oh gosh, oh gosh, let me through." Annabelle bent down and put one hand behind Mary's head. Mary's face was screwed up. "Mary, Mary, are you alright?" Annabelle said in a whisper.

Mary let out a long exhale. "I'm fine, Annabelle. Just leave me here. You go . . ."

"I can't leave you here!"

Mary screwed up her face again. After a minute, she relaxed. "Of course, you can. You have to get married."

Annabelle's head popped up. "Harper! We need you!" Harper's face burst into the huddle. "She's all yours."

For the first time, Harper's expression was fearful. "But I'm a pathologist!"

"You're a doctor. Improvise. Beside, it'll be good for you to be at the other end of the life cycle for a change. Look, there's a manger over there." Annabelle pointed to a cattle trough. "It's a sign."

"If it was good enough for Jesus, it'll be good enough for my baby," Mary said. She giggled, her pink cheeks shining. Then she gasped. "Ow!"

Harper gently took Mary's hand from Annabelle's. "Alright, off you go, Annabelle. I'll take over here. Mike's waiting for you."

CHAPTER FIFTY-TWO

THE ATMOSPHERE IN the church amongst the wedding guests had changed dramatically in the hour they had been waiting. On taking their seats, hushed chatter and excitement had bubbled amongst them. But as time passed, the absence of several significant female guests, the disappearance of the groom, and the non-appearance of the bride caused the crowd to get restless. They began to impatiently check their watches and cross their arms, muttering amongst themselves until almost every single one of them had run out of excuses for the lack of action.

They had mostly given up on any pretence at patience and decorum, twisting in their seats and casually standing up to stretch as they chatted loudly with each other. A few of them tutted and rolled their eyes as they remarked upon how they had expected better. Outside, villagers spread their picnic blankets between gravestones and got out sandwiches and thermos.

"I told my wife these things never start on time," John Boldrick, the postman, said to the person sitting next to him.

"Even she's not here. I gave up waiting for her and came on my own."

"What do you think is holding them up?" an old man said from the pew in front.

The postman shrugged. "A rip in her dress? Bridesmaids got into a fight? Who knows?"

"Cold feet," the woman to his side said. "Annabelle's changed her mind. The poor inspector. So humiliating for him."

In the small, secluded church office, there was even more trepidation and tension as Father John tried to assuage the groom. "Perhaps we should go back out there," Father John said, watching the inspector pace from one end of the small room to the other. "It might calm the guests a little."

"It won't calm me very much!" Mike said. Father John could almost see exasperation radiating off him.

"Look, I'm sure she's just late."

"I saw the clues," Mike said, shaking his head. "The way she kept putting off the preparations. That she thought she might have to move to Truro. The witch's vision . . ."

"The witch's what?" Father John said.

"Never mind," dismissed Mike. "But I thought it was all done and dusted. That her hesitation was gone."

"Look, let's just go out there and make some small talk. Buy ourselves a little time."

"She's not coming," Mike said. "I know it. She's jilting me at the altar."

"Come now, Inspector. You're talking nonsense, and you know it."

"Nonsense? We haven't even had a call from Derbyshire! He's probably chased her halfway to London by now! If it's just a silly delay, why didn't she send a message before running off? And why is she running? Was marriage to me such an awful prospect?"

Father John sighed. He had run out of excuses for Annabelle. His hope that there had been a misunderstanding had mostly left him. He prayed for resolution.

Mike looked at his watch again. "That's it," Mike said.

"Where are you going?"

"Where do you think?! I'm going out there to tell everyone the wedding's off," Mike said as he yanked the door open.

"Wait! Mike! No!" Father John cried, quickly following him as the younger man marched out to face the chattering crowd. "There must be a good reason for Annabelle to do this. How about we try understanding before being hasty? This isn't the action of the woman you love, of Annabelle, now is it?"

But Mike wasn't listening. The hubbub in the church quietened at the sight of him, the tense, stern expression on the inspector's face alarming the more observant guests who'd become used to his more relaxed features in recent months. Mike walked to the spot where Father John should have been pronouncing him and Annabelle husband and wife. Instead, Father John stood beside him nervously wringing his hands, uttering a silent prayer.

Mike opened his mouth to speak to the guests. There was a huge bang as the double doors of the church slammed open. The guests gasped. They spun around to see what, or who, could have swept the doors open with such powerful force. There, at the church doors, silhouetted against the bright morning light, stood Philippa. She was wearing a remarkable pink dress bought specially for the wedding and a matching wide-brimmed hat. Even more remarkable were the stains and flecks of grass on her skirt. There was mud on her pink satin shoes. Her hat was battered and askew. A streak of dirt ran down her cheek.

Despite these uncharacteristic sartorial failures, Philippa confidently walked up to the front of the church where Mike and Father John were standing. The church fell deathly silent. "There's been a minor incident," Philippa said to Mike with the commanding tone she usually reserved for her knitting circle. "Nothing to worry about. The wedding will begin in precisely one hour."

CHAPTER FIFTY-THREE

PHILIPPA DID NOT wait for responses or objections. Her message delivered, after a quick word to Mary's and Harper's husbands, who immediately dashed from their pews, she walked back down the aisle, her head high. She allowed the giant oak doors to swing closed behind her, leaving the astonished guests to pick up their jaws and lower their eyebrows. Uncomfortable, several of them began to examine the order of service in minute detail as though nothing had happened whilst murmurs rose from the others as they began to discuss the situation.

There was good reason for Philippa's brevity. Back at the cottage was a crowd of women whose muddy, dirtied dresses needed to be returned to pristine, wedding-photo-worthy condition.

In her many years as church secretary, Philippa had performed several acts of Herculean proportions under heavy duress. There was the time when Annabelle had a meeting with the bishop on a bank holiday and had forgotten to tell her that he was vegetarian. She'd had to create a veggie buffet for nineteen with nothing but the remnants of her fridge and two hours. There was the time she had to bake two hundred cupcakes in one morning to replace those eaten by Biscuit and Magic who, having eaten most of them, fell asleep on the rest. And then she'd had to laminate thirty-four winners' certificates for the church fête competitions with half an hour to spare after the originals were inadvertently left in the church hall kitchen and the children's playgroup leaders had used them as table mats at snack time. But the challenge Philippa now faced was greater than them all.

She marched back into the cottage where the women were still chattering and giggling with relief and excitement over their cross-country manhunt. She clapped her hands loudly. "Right! Everyone undress! Now!" Unquestioningly, the women began to do as Philippa ordered, finding it one of the less surprising demands that had been asked of them all day.

"Samira," Philippa commanded. "Get the basins. There's one in the bathroom, one in the garden, and one under the sink in the kitchen. Fill them with warm water, then take them outside." Samira quickly disappeared. "Katie, get the ironing board from the passage cupboard and set it up. Mrs. Dixon, as mother of the bride, you go first. There's a clothes press in the shed; the key is on the desk by the door there. Mrs. Shoreditch, there's a sewing kit over by the television. Mrs. Applebury, tend to any injuries. The first aid kit is on the shelf in the cupboard under the stairs. Barbara, give me a hand with these buttons. The rest of you, take your clothes outside and start scraping!"

"Surely we should use a washing machine?" Gabriella said.

"A quick wash, a quick dry, and they should be fine,"

Sophie added.

"Are you quite mad?" Philippa said, glaring at the women as if they'd just said the daftest thing she'd ever heard, which in fact they had. "With these fabrics? And this many clothes? No. There's only one way we're going to get all this sorted, and that's the old-fashioned way—a quick repair, a spot wash, and a press."

"Um, Philippa?" Mrs. Shoreditch said quietly.

"Yes?"

"Why do I need the sewing kit? I don't think anyone's dress is damaged, just dirty."

"Stay there, Mrs. Shoreditch."

Philippa walked over to Annabelle, clutched her by the shoulders, and walked her back to Mrs. Shoreditch. Annabelle's tiara was halfway down the back of her head. Her veil was ripped, a seam at the shoulder of her dress had torn, and there was a big streak of mud down the back of the skirt. She looked like she had been rampaging through the British countryside in her wedding dress. Which indeed she had.

Philippa pointed at Annabelle's mud-covered skirt. "The best dry-cleaner in the land would need at least two days to clean that much dirt from that amount of delicate fabric. It's impossible. This dress needs a complete rethink. And you have"—Philippa looked at her watch—"fifty-three minutes to do it."

Annabelle caught sight of herself in the full-length mirror. She gasped. "What are we going to do? I am completely in your hands, Philippa. Tell me what to do and I will do it."

Philippa's eyes softened. Her knees went weak. They were words she had thought she would never hear. Philippa placed a gentle hand on Annabelle's shoulder, her eyes sympathetic but gleaming. "We're going to have to cut it off."

"Cut it off?!" Annabelle exclaimed. "You want to cut my dress to pieces?"

"It's the only way," Philippa said sadly.

"But you'll ruin it!" Annabelle exclaimed.

"We take that risk, or you walk down the aisle looking like you've been wrestling pigs, Reverend," Philippa said.

"Fortune does favour the brave, love," Mrs. Dixon said.

Annabelle's heart sank. "Do you think you can do it, Mrs. Shoreditch? Do you think it'll look alright?" Mrs. Shoreditch gulped so loudly everyone could hear.

"Of course she can!" Philippa said proudly. "This is Mrs. Shoreditch! She can do anything with a needle and thread and some scissors! Did you see that cocktail dress she made for last year's Christmas raffle? Now, let's go! We've got a church full of people waiting!"

What ensued was a flurry of activity the likes of which 101-year-old Mrs. Politely, who was sitting quietly in the corner out of the way, had not seen since wartime. The women (wo)manned their stations and cut, cleaned, pressed, and dressed with the precision, urgency, and focus they had never attached to any task ever before. They had fifty-three minutes after which, well, who knew, but they had fifty-three minutes. Even Gabriella and Sophie stopped twittering.

With five minutes to go, and after a few panics, minor emergencies, and some defeated objections, the women finished restoring their wedding wardrobes. With their clothes back on, now in near-perfect condition if you didn't look too closely or around the back, they marvelled at what they had achieved. Annabelle in her new, improved, and completely stain-free wedding dress stood amidst them all.

"It's a miracle worthy of a sainthood!" Barbara complimented Mrs. Shoreditch.

"I think your dress suits you better now," Mrs. Dixon said.

"All that running around probably burned off a few pounds!" Philippa added. "What do you think, Reverend?"

Annabelle turned this way and that in the mirror, ignoring Sophie and Gabriella, who beseeched her to stay still as they stuck tiny false eyelashes at the edges of her eyelids and dotted pale pink lipstick on her lips. Tracy from the local hairdressers wielded a steaming curling iron. "I think it looks sensational!" Annabelle fair gleamed—her cheeks as shiny as her eyes.

Mrs. Shoreditch had detached the muddy, full, silk overskirt and lace petticoats from the bodice, unpicked the stained panels from the clean ones, and sewn up the skirt once more so that Annabelle's silhouette was now streamlined and elegant. She had removed the lace from Annabelle's shoulders so that they and her arms were now bare. Her tiara and veil had proved irredeemable, so Mrs. Applebury quickly wove a headpiece from pink cherry blossom and foliage she found in the garden. Tracey fixed it in Annabelle's now wavy hair.

Annabelle's satin wedding shoes had remained pristine. The same couldn't be said for her pedicure, which was now a complete disaster, but Philippa reminded her no one would notice. When Annabelle put the shoes on, the small heel transformed Annabelle's gait from galumphing to graceful.

Philippa beamed. "Are you ready to get married, my lady?"

Annabelle laughed. "Absolutely. I had no idea getting married would be the easiest thing I had to do today!"

CHAPTER FIFTY-FOUR

THE WOMEN, THEIR outfits reinvigorated, left the cottage arm in arm and walked to the church. There, they dispersed to take their seats amongst the quiet, expectant crowd. Bonnie, Felicity, and ring-bearer Dougie left with Mrs. Dixon to await the bride at the church entrance. Philippa and Barbara helped Mrs. Polightly out of her seat in the cottage and slowly guided her to a comfy chair that had been placed at the front of the church especially for her.

"You look grand, love." Annabelle's father took her hands in his, his eyes moist. He looked into his daughter's eyes. He'd waited quietly in the pub until he'd been needed and was blissfully unaware of the drama that had taken place in the cottage, the countryside, and the church. "You've come a long way."

"Oh, Dad. I know I'm doing the right thing, but I'm a bit scared."

"Perfectly normal, love. I was terrified when I married your mum. Now look at me, decades later. We've had our hard times and weathered a lot, but we've done it as a team. And that's what Mike and you'll do too.

"I know, but . . ."

"Listen, do you remember that day I left you at university? You were scared then, too, worried about the change. A month later, it was like you'd been there all your life!" He gave her a light kiss on the cheek so as not to mess up her makeup. Annabelle smiled, her eyes glittering with unshed tears. She silently nodded. Raymond Dixon dug into his pocket and pulled out a crumpled paper bag. "Toffee?"

Annabelle left the cottage with her father. The crowds on their picnic blankets turned as they heard the church gate creak open. They stood silently as Annabelle passed. She and her father stopped briefly to look over at old Mr. Austin's giant headstone standing proud and tall in the graveyard. Annabelle smiled when she saw it, remembering the mysterious church benefactor's desire to be buried in the village that had harboured him quietly after his escape from his enemies. Feeling content and at peace, Annabelle and her father continued on to join the children at the church entrance. Mrs. Dixon shushed their giggling and got them into place. Annabelle and her mother exchanged a warm gaze. Her father held out his arm for his daughter. "Ready?"

"Ready." They faced forwards to look along the aisle to the front of the church. All Annabelle could see of Mike was his broad shoulders that gave no hint of his earlier anxiety. Chantelle looked over her shoulder and murmured in Mike's ear. Father John smiled encouragingly. He winked at Annabelle.

The organist played the first notes of the wedding processional. The air filled with the honey-thick sounds full of love and warmth, sombre and serious, along with the rustling of the congregation as they stood to welcome the bridal party. The atmosphere pulsed with energy. Annabelle could almost see electrical charges zapping through the air as the wedding guests stared ahead, anticipating the first sight of her after their long wait. Some turned their heads surreptitiously, unable to be patient.

As Annabelle moved through the church, rays of light filtered through the stained glass windows and landed on the floor before her, lighting her way with a kaleidoscope of colour. Her guests gasped at the sight of her transformed from humble cleric to radiant beauty. Eyelashes fluttered, and tears were batted away. Annabelle drew level with Mike at the top of the aisle. He smiled; she blushed.

Annabelle's father stood to one side, and Annabelle gazed into Mike's eyes. The organ stopped, and Father John began. For Annabelle, the ceremony occurred in a dream-like state. It seemed too perfect, too beautiful, and too much like the way she had imagined for it to be real. But when Mike said "I do," his voice unmistakably strong, she knew it was true. And when she spoke her vows clearly and without hesitation, she was sure of it.

Father John's smile grew an inch wider. He instructed them to place the rings fashioned from Cornish gold on one another's fingers and said to Mike, "You may now kiss the bride."

The cheer started outside the church, the entrance acting like a funnel, concentrating the sound as it passed through, picking up speed and volume as it made its way up the aisle to the couple. For a few seconds, Annabelle wasn't sure whether the explosion of sound and movement was in her head or happening around her, but when she and Mike broke apart, she saw people standing, clapping, and cheering.

Mike laughed and took her hand, and they almost leapt down the aisle. Smiling at the congregation, they passed through the church entrance before stopping in surprise. On both sides of the church path were police officers, truncheons aloft, tips touching to form an arch. Constable Raven was there along with Derbyshire, Jenny McAllister back from maternity leave, Harris, and Colback. Even Chambers and Rose had returned from secondment to other forces for the day. But when she looked closer, Annabelle noticed that shoulder to shoulder with the officers were protectors of a quite different kind. Dylan, the bear-man, was the first person Annabelle recognised, and then as she looked, she saw that every other guard was a traveller. Their arches were formed from sticks, each decorated with pink flowers and green vines undoubtedly pulled from the woods they camped next to. A guard of honour had assembled.

After pauses to smile for Barney Slimmer, the photographer, happy, familiar voices encouraged them down the church path towards the glorious, gleaming Rolls Royce, the door of which Ted Lovesey was holding open for them. As Mike and Annabelle ran through the guard of honour to Ted's car, confetti rained down like multicoloured sprinkles.

They climbed into the back of the car, then looked out of the window at the crowd of faces blowing them kisses and waving happily, a few of them brushing away tears. The car moved off slowly, the church and the crowd disappearing in the rear window, finally leaving the newly married couple alone.

"What a day," Annabelle said, sighing. "I'm so happy!"

Mike nodded and smiled at his bride, still holding her hands in his. A slight frown appeared on his face, however. "But why were you so late? I was moments away from calling the whole thing off! I thought you'd jilted me at the altar. I thought I was playing a part in some obscure independent art film."

Annabelle chuckled. "I'm so terribly sorry, Mike," she said. "But I was doing your job for you. Consider the case of Kathleen's witch murder solved."

Flabbergasted, Mike said, "What? You mean you caught the killer?"

"With some help," Annabelle said. "I couldn't have you worrying about an open case throughout our honeymoon now, could I?"

"How? When? Who?" Mike said, the questions in his mind flowing too quickly for words.

"Oh, there'll be plenty of time to explain later. For now, I'm only interested in committing my own sinful act with you."

"What?"

"Cutting a white chocolate and lemon wedding cake and eating as much of it as I want!"

CHAPTER FIFTY-FIVE

AT WOODLANDS MANOR, the newlyweds were greeted by two guests who had been absent from the wedding—their dogs, Molly and Magic. Biscuit, naturally, was absent. She had been unwilling to cooperate, and Philippa hadn't wanted to ruin her dress tussling with a disgruntled cat. The dogs had been well looked after during the wedding by gardener Alfred Roper, who'd been pruning, cutting, and watering until the very last minute so that the grounds were perfect. Soon the Rolls Royce was joined by a battalion of other vehicles as they filtered into the grounds of the large mansion, carrying the rest of the guests who mingled and offered further congratulations to the couple as they were plied with champagne. As the reason for Annabelle's delayed appearance spread, it took a while for everyone to settle in their seats.

Once a glass of champagne had been placed into his hand, Mike finally allowed himself to relax, believing that all his troubles were behind him. It was at that moment he noticed Derbyshire walking across the grounds towards him.

"Sir!"

"Oh, not again," Mike said, gulping down his champagne and looking around for a refill. He noticed the tall, thin man with a hangdog expression beside Derbyshire and suddenly wondered if he'd drunk too much already.

"Neil? Derbyshire! What are you doing bringing a criminal to my wedding? Are you mad, man?"

"It's okay, Mike," Annabelle said as she walked up to him, placing a calming hand on his arm, a gesture she suspected she might be using quite often in the coming decades. "I invited him."

"You did? Why on earth would you do that?"

Annabelle looked from her husband to the intense young man who had berated her from a log. "I know why you felt so angry towards me, Neil," Annabelle said. "I found out about that incident at your ministry. You wanted to be ordained, but during your training, you broke the main altar piece when you were cleaning it, didn't you?" Neil hung his head. "You were kicked out—by a female priest."

"It was a bad decision," Neil mumbled.

"I agree," Annabelle said. Neil looked up at Annabelle curiously. "So, I spoke to Father John about you. I can't offer you a path to the priesthood, but if you're willing to move to London, then Father John assures me he will find a place for you to serve. The churches there are in dire need. It will be hard work. But Father John is a patient man, an excellent priest, and a wonderful mentor. And he knows how to get the best out of clumsy people." Annabelle smiled. "If you're willing, he will guide you back onto the path you fell from."

Neil looked up at Annabelle in astonishment. "Are you serious?"

"Absolutely. I think you're a good man, Neil. You have strong faith and conviction, which is a great asset, though it can be an enormous burden and a force for destruction when directed poorly. Nonetheless, forgiveness is the Lord's message, not least the capacity to forgive oneself."

Neil gawped for a few seconds, as if words had been stolen from his mouth. "I-I . . . Thank you," he managed finally. "Wow, I never thought anyone would help me. Least of all, a woman priest."

Annabelle chuckled. "That's the burden of a closed mind. Today is a day for open hearts. A new beginning, eh? Now get along; we've got a cake to eat."

With the guests now settling into their seats, the first plates being carried out for serving, Annabelle stopped quickly at Sophie and Gabriella's table.

"Ladies," Annabelle said, gaining their attention.

"Oh, Reverend! Hello!"

"What an exciting day!"

"Yes! All action!"

"Chasing a criminal and attending a wedding!"

"All those hunky men on horses and such!"

"And it's not even two o'clock!"

Annabelle laughed gently as she stood between their chairs. "I have a favour to ask you," she said. "Would you deliver some of the food and perhaps a lot of cake to the travellers' camp?"

"The gypsies!" exclaimed a man from across the table. "Why-ever would you do that?"

Annabelle looked mildly over at the speaker. Nothing would faze her today. "Because without those wonderful people, Harper would be in a terrible state, and I would not be married. I want to show my appreciation."

"But you already are," Sophie said.

"Look outside," Gabriella added.

Annabelle looked across the marquee to the lawn.

There, sitting down on picnic blankets and in deckchairs, chatting to their neighbours, were the villagers. Mixed amongst them were travellers. Annabelle watched the villagers sharing their food, handing around sandwiches and sharing cups of tea, everyone laughing and joking as though they had been friends for years. From a distance, Dylan and Jonquil quietly nodded at her. Annabelle nodded back.

To many it felt like both an apt ending and a wonderful beginning. Having shared so much of the vicar's life these past few years, having seen the trials she had overcome and the efforts she had invested in the community, seeing her so undeniably, gloriously happy felt as if something slightly askew had been put right, order had been restored, and justice had been served. And not a single person in that reception tent could deny that this was anything less than the good vicar deserved.

CHAPTER FIFTY-SIX

A CHORUS OF oohs and aahs greeted the ivory wedding cake, a five-layered masterpiece decorated with purple flowers. It had been a joint effort between Katie Flynn and Mike's sister, Chantelle. They had been collaborating in secret for weeks but had only realised their vision for the cake a few hours ago. The two women were as much relieved as delighted that things had gone to plan, not to mention they were exhausted.

On each layer, in intricate fondant detail, they had depicted scenes from Annabelle's and Mike's lives—the church, the police, their animals, their love, and finally their marriage. Real flowers selected from those grown for the wedding in village gardens snaked up the cake and culminated in a topper that Chantelle had designed: a combination of the police badge, the cross, and a heart. Phone cameras whirred and cheers punctuated the air as Annabelle and Mike cut the cake and posed for pictures, their beaming smiles illuminating the photos before they kissed and handed out pieces of what was indisputably the finest wedding cake Upton St. Mary had ever seen.

After plates were cleaned and second helpings deployed, silence descended on the room. It was time for the speeches and toasts. Mike, Annabelle, Chantelle, and Annabelle's father all delivered heartfelt words of hope, happiness, and in Annabelle's father's case, utter relief.

Even Philippa spoke. The small woman stood up from her position a few seats down the top table from Annabelle. She raised her glass, and the room went silent. "I remember, years ago now, sitting in the kitchen of the reverend's cottage and telling her what a lovely couple she and the inspector would make. 'A vicar and a police inspector,' I said, 'like something from a novel!' Our vicar dismissed it, saying, 'I'm in no rush to begin courting, thank you.' Well, she changed her mind, but she certainly took her time!" The crowd laughed. "But that's Annabelle for you: patient, content, happy-go-lucky. I have worked with the reverend every day since she first came to Upton St. Mary. I've only seen her get upset at other people's suffering. I've only seen her strive to make life better for others. She's never asked for much herself, but she's done everything she can to make this village a thriving, bustling, harmonious community. So, it feels right that she now has someone by her side to make her happy, someone to look after her as much as she has looked after all of us."

The crowd nodded, murmurs of agreement humming around the marquee. A few men banged their palms on the table in approval.

"Many thought this wedding would never happen. And I must admit, when I was chasing Annabelle across the fields ten minutes before the ceremony was to start, I began to have doubts myself. But that's what life with the reverend is like: never dull, sometimes exciting, and always with our best interests in mind. Possibly the most important piece of advice I can give the inspector is that to live with Annabelle you must have energy, compassion, and your wits about you. Fortunately, he has all these things, and I couldn't imagine a better husband for my wonderful friend." The crowd clapped wildly as Annabelle acknowledged Philippa's words and the guests' approval with a beaming smile.

Just when it seemed the marquee could not contain any more joy, a cry went up and everyone turned to see Mary—bedraggled, straw in her hair, her cheeks even pinker than ever—standing at the door to the marquee. She was still wearing her matron of honour dress.

"Mary!" Annabelle cried when she saw her. She rushed over, stopping abruptly as she reached her friend. Mary smiled shyly. In her arms was a tiny, sleeping baby. "Good grief, Mary! What did you do? Squat down in a field like in olden times?"

"Pretty much. The travellers showed me how. And Harper was a big help. We're going to call her Belle, Annabelle. After you."

Another cheer went up. There were more popped corks, more cheers, and even more reasons to smile. The guests resumed their excited chatter, but it lasted only a few minutes before a loud, rhythmic rumble grew in volume. The sides of the tent flapped as if a hurricane were breaking against them. Tent ropes sprung from the ground with a force that could cause a nasty sting. The ceiling began to ripple.

"What's going on?"

"Is there a thunderstorm?"

"Oh my word!"

Guests clutched at their tables, casting surprised looks at each other as they searched for some explanation. They looked outside, confused by the lack of rain. It was still a beautiful day, but the crowd outside was looking into the sky as empty deckchairs flew around them.

"Come on," Mike said to Annabelle with a mischievous smile. "That's our cue."

Annabelle faced him for a moment before a look of understanding crept over her face. "Mike! You didn't!"

"I did," Mike said, standing up and offering his hand.

CHAPTER FIFTY-SEVEN

MIKE LED ANNABELLE in quick strides to the exit, their guests getting up from their seats to follow them outside.

The helicopter gracefully lowered itself onto the empty lawn beside the marquee. The downforce of its rotors flattened the grass whilst the guests clutched their hats as they squinted at the scene in wonder. Molly and Magic barked at the intruder with excitement as the chopper landed softly, spinning around at the last moment to present its doors to the bride and groom.

After they hurriedly bade farewell to their families, Philippa, and Mary, Mike and Annabelle ran hand in hand to the helicopter, turning once to wave at the crowd. "See you after the honeymoon!" Mike shouted above the noise, wrapping an arm around Annabelle to guide her inside.

As soon as they were buckled up, the helicopter swept upwards, angling itself so that the newly married couple looked down on the crowd as they made a quick circle of the guests. Mike and Annabelle waved through the window before the pilot gave the engine full throttle and they hurtled towards the early evening horizon.

"Oh, Mike!" Annabelle gasped. "You really are full of surprises!"

Mike chuckled. "A trait we share, I think."

"We'll be there in an hour," the pilot called over his shoulder.

"Where? Mike, where are we going?"

"Jersey," Mike said warmly to his bride. "Channel Islands."

"I've always wanted to go there." Annabelle sighed. "I never thought I'd be doing it with my husband, though."

Mike laughed and put an arm around Annabelle's shoulders. "We're staying in a pretty little fishing town."

"But what about the case? Do you have to clear anything up? Cross some t's, dot some i's?"

"I'll file a report when I get there. Gorey's got a pretty efficient team. Good cleanup rate. Lead detective—David Graham—is a bit of a legend."

Annabelle snuggled into Mike's chest and lay her head on his shoulder. Up ahead, as they hurtled towards the horizon, the flup-flup-flup sounds of the helicopter rotator blades thudded above them and pink clouds peppered a blue sky. The sun was beginning to set.

"Red sky at night, shepherd's delight," Annabelle murmured.

"What?"

"Red sky at night, shepherd's delight," she repeated. "Tomorrow's going to be a lovely day."

Annabelle thought about her parents, her brother Roger and his daughter Bonnie. Back at the reception, her mother would be kicking back, chatting to Philippa, enjoying a glass of champagne. Her father would finally be relaxing after the stress of making his speech. Bonnie would be getting tired and Roger thinking of putting her to bed. Her friend Mary would be feeding her baby whilst Father John anticipated his long drive back to London the next day. Annabelle took a deep breath and relaxed her shoulders as she exhaled. She closed her eyes.

When she saw her family and friends again, she would be a married woman with some experience of what marriage entailed. For there was no doubt that stretching in front of her, more adventures lay. Adventures that, like those pink clouds in an unending blue sky, promised joy, pleasure, and for shepherds like her, hard work and the satisfaction of a job well done. One chapter was closing, another just beginning.

"I can't wait," she murmured.

"For what?" Mike asked.

"For the rest of my life. With you, God," she shifted in her seat. "And cake."

Thank you for reading *Witches at the Wedding*! It's time to leave Annabelle and Mike in peace to get on with their lives. Annabelle is a little piece of me and it is bittersweet to say goodbye but I'm so happy that she is beloved and the series is in a good place. I'm also excited to have the time to write new characters in other series. To find out about new books, sign up for my newsletter: https://www.alisongolden.com

If you love the Reverend Annabelle series, you'll want to read the *USA Today* bestselling Inspector Graham series featuring a new and unusual detective with a phenomenal memory and a tragic past. The first in the series, *The Case of the Screaming Beauty* is available for purchase from Amazon and FREE in Kindle Unlimited..

And don't miss the Roxy Reinhardt mysteries. Will Roxy triumph after her life falls apart? She's sacked from her job, her boyfriend dumps her, she's out of money. So, on a whim, she goes on the trip of a lifetime to New Orleans, There, she gets mixed up in a Mardi Gras murder. *Things were going to be fine. They were, weren't they?* Get the first in the series, Mardi Gras Madness from Amazon. Also FREE in Kindle Unlimited!

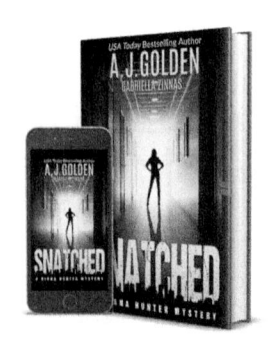

If you're looking for something edgy and dangerous, root for Diana Hunter as she seeks justice after a devastating crime destroys her family. Start following her journey in this non-stop series of suspense and action. The first book in the series, Snatched is available to buy on Amazon and is FREE in Kindle Unlimited.

I hugely appreciate your help in spreading the word about *Witches at the Wedding,* including telling a friend.

Reviews help readers find books! Please leave a review on your favourite book site.

Turn the page for an excerpt from the first book in the Inspector David Graham series, *The Case of the Screaming Beauty* . . .

ALISON GOLDEN
Grace Dagnall

USA Today Bestselling Author

AN INSPECTOR DAVID GRAHAM MYSTERY

The Case of the
Screaming Beauty

THE CASE OF THE SCREAMING BEAUTY
CHAPTER ONE

AMELIA SWANSBOURNE STRAIGHTENED up, wincing slightly, and admired the freshly weeded flower bed with an almost professional pride. It was, she mused, as though she were fighting a continuous, low-level war against insidious intruders whose intentions were not only to take root and flourish, but whose impact on the impeccably arranged beds and rockeries of her garden was as unwelcome as a hurricane. Amelia was ruthless and precise, going about her work with a methodical focus that reminded her of those "gardening monks" she'd once seen in a documentary. Perhaps, she chuckled, moving onto the next flower bed, weeding would be her path to enlightenment.

As she knelt on her cushioned, flower-patterned pad and began the familiar rhythm once more, she let her mind go where it wanted. How many other women in their early sixties, she wondered, were carrying out this basic, time-honoured task at this very moment? She pictured those quiet English gardens being lovingly tended on this very temperate Sunday morning, silently wishing her fellow gardeners a peaceful and productive couple of hours. It must have been true, though, that she faced a larger and more demanding test than most. The gardens of the Lavender Inn were spread over an impressive and endlessly challenging four and a half acres.

Guests loved walking in the gardens. They had become a major attraction for many of the city folk who retreated from London to this country idyll. Amongst the visitors were those all-important ones who checked in under false names, and then, after their visit was over, went back to their computers to write online reviews, the power of which could make or break a bed and breakfast like the Lavender. The gardens appeared often in comments on those review websites, so Amelia knew her work was an investment, however time-consuming it could be. Keeping the gardens in check—not only weeded but watered, constantly improved, pruned, fed, and composted—would have been a full-time job for any experienced gardener, but Amelia handled virtually all of the guesthouse's horticultural needs on her own. She preferred it this way, but it did take its toll. Not least on her ageing knees.

The gardens had proved such a draw and the satisfaction of their splendid appearance was so great that Amelia had long ago judged her efforts to be very much worthwhile. Besides, it was a fitting, ongoing tribute to her late Uncle Terry, who had bequeathed Amelia and her husband this remarkable Tudor building and its gardens. The sudden inheritance had come as quite a shock. Cliff, in particular, was worried that he was entirely unready to be the co-host of a popular and high-end B&B. However, Terry had no children and had been as much a father to Amelia as had her own. It made her proud and happy to believe that the place was being run well and that the gardens had become the envy of the village of Chiddlinghurst, and, judging by those reviews, beyond.

A bed of roses formed the easterly flank of the main quadrangle, within which Amelia had spent much of the morning. They were looking particularly lovely; three crimson and scarlet varieties found their natural partners in the lily-white species which bloomed opposite on the western side. By the house itself, an imposing Tudor mansion with all its old, dark, wood beams still intact, there were smaller beds and a rockery on either side of a spacious patio with white, cast-iron lawn furniture. Further over, against the western wing of the inn, was a bed of which Amelia was particularly proud: deep-green ferns and low-light flowering plants, their lush colours providing a quick dose of restful ease amongst the brighter hues around them. Amelia took a moment to let the greens sink into her mind, soothing and promising in equal measure. She indulged in a deep, nourishing breath and began truly to relax and enjoy her morning in the garden. Which was why the piercing scream that burst from the open window of the room just above the bed of ferns turned Amelia's blood as cold as ice.

Dropping her trowel and shedding her heavy work gloves, Amelia dashed across the immaculate lawn of the quadrangle and up the four stone steps that led to the patio. Peering through the conservatory doors, she could see nothing out of place. She was quickly through and into the dining room and then the lobby. She took the stairs as fast as her ailing knees would allow, and within seconds of hearing the scream, she was knocking at the door of a guest room.

"Mrs. Travis? Can you hear me? Is everything alright?" Amelia panted, her mind already racing ahead to the horrors that might accompany some kind of tragedy at this popular house.

"Mrs. Travis?" she repeated, raising her hand to knock once more.

The door opened and Norah Travis was smiling placidly. "Hello, Amelia. Whatever is the matter?"

"You're alright!" Amelia observed with a great sigh of relief. "Good heavens above, I feared something awful had happened."

"I'm sure I don't know what you mean," Norah assured her. "It's been a pretty quiet Sunday morning, so far."

There was nothing about Norah which might raise any kind of alarm. As usual, there wasn't a blonde hair out of place, and her bright blue eyes were gleaming. If anything, Amelia decided, she looked even younger than her twenty-seven years.

"I could have sworn," Amelia told her, gradually regaining her breath, "that I heard a scream from the window there," she pointed, "whilst I was outside in the garden. Clear as day."

"Oh, I've nothing to scream about, Amelia," Norah replied. "Could it have been someone else? I don't think I heard anything."

Cliff won't let me hear the end of this. He'll say I'm losing my marbles, that I've finally gone loopy. And who's to say he's wrong? "It must have been, my dear. I'm so sorry to have disturbed you."

Amelia bid Norah a good morning and returned downstairs, distracted by the chilling memory of the sound, as well as its mysterious origin. She could have sworn on a stack of Bibles....

To get your copy of The Case of the Screaming Beauty visit the link below:
https://www.alisongolden.com/screaming-beauty

REVERENTIAL RECIPES

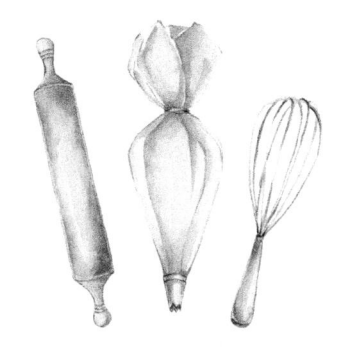

Continue on to check out the recipes for goodies featured in this book...

PASSIONATE PLUM CHARLOTTE

Approx. 2 oz (60g) butter
6 oz (170g) fresh white breadcrumbs
1 ½ lb (700g) ripe fresh plums, halved and stoned
4 oz (115g) soft brown sugar
Finely grated rind and juice of ½ lemon
7½ fl oz (225ml) fresh or diluted frozen orange juice

Preheat the oven to 190°C/375°F/Gas Mark 5. Brush the base and sides of a shallow baking dish with some of the butter. Cover the base with some of the breadcrumbs.

Put a layer of plums in the dish, sprinkle with some of the sugar and a little lemon rind and juice. Dot with more butter. Continue with these layers until all the ingredients are used up, finishing with a layer of breadcrumbs and dotting with butter.

Pour over the orange juice and bake in a fairly hot oven for 40 to 45 minutes or until the Charlotte feels tender when pierced with a skewer and the top layer of breadcrumbs is golden-brown. Serve straight from the baking dish. **Serves 4 to 6.**

CONTEMPLATIVE CUSTARD TART

For the shortcrust pastry
4 oz (115g) flour
Pinch of salt
1 tbsp sugar
2 oz (60g) butter
1-2 tbsp water

For the custard
2 eggs, beaten
1 oz (30g) sugar
½ pint (235ml) milk
½ tsp grated nutmeg

Preheat the oven to 200°C/400°F/Gas Mark 6. To prepare the pastry, sift the flour and salt into a mixing bowl, then stir in the sugar. Add the butter in pieces and rub into the flour until the mixture resembles fine breadcrumbs.

Gradually stir in enough water to form a soft dough. Form the dough into a ball and wrap in foil or greaseproof paper. Chill in the refrigerator for 30 minutes.

Roll out the chilled dough on a floured board to a circle large enough to line a 18cm/7 inch flan dish placed on a baking sheet. Prick the bottom of the dough. Chill in the refrigerator for a further 15 minutes.

Meanwhile, make the custard. Put the eggs and sugar in a mixing bowl and beat in the milk with a fork until the sugar dissolves. Strain the custard into the chilled flan case.

Sprinkle with grated nutmeg and bake in the preheated oven for 10 minutes. Lower the heat to 180°C/350°F/Gas Mark 4, and bake for a further 20 to 25 minutes or until the pastry is golden and the filling is set.

Serve warm or cold.

JOYOUS JAM ROLY-POLY

4 oz (115g) self-raising flour
¾ tsp baking powder
Pinch of salt
2 oz (60g) shredded beef suet or shortening
2-3 tbsp hot water
8 tbsp jam

Sift the flour and salt into a mixing bowl. Stir in the suet or shortening, then gradually stir in the hot water until the dough comes together and leaves the sides of the bowl. Knead until smooth, then roll out on a floured board to an oblong about 0.5cm/¼-inch thick.

Spread half of the jam along the dough, leaving a margin round the sides. Roll up like a Swiss roll from one of the short ends, pinching and sealing the edges with a little water. Wrap loosely in greased foil or a double thickness of greaseproof paper. Seal well.

Place in the top of a steamer over rapidly boiling water and steam for 1½ to 2 hours, topping up the water level from time to time during cooking.

Just before serving the roly-poly, heat the remaining jam in a small pan. When the roly-poly is cooked, remove from the steamer, unwrap the foil or greaseproof paper and transfer the pudding to a hot serving dish. Pour over the warmed jam and serve immediately with custard, cream, or ice cream. **Serves 3 to 4.**

All ingredients are available from your local store or online retailer.

You can find printable versions of these recipes at www.alisongolden.com/wwrecipes

"Your emails seem to come on days when I need to read them because they are so upbeat."
- Linda W -

For a limited time, you can get the first books in each of my series - *Chaos in Cambridge, Hunted* (exclusively for subscribers - not available anywhere else), *The Case of the Screaming Beauty,* and *Mardi Gras Madness* - plus updates about new releases, promotions, and other Insider exclusives, by signing up for my mailing list at:

https://www.alisongolden.com/annabelle

TAKE MY QUIZ

What kind of mystery reader are you? Take my thirty second quiz to find out!

https://www.alisongolden.com/quiz

BOOKS IN THE REVEREND ANNABELLE DIXON SERIES

Chaos in Cambridge (Prequel)

Death at the Café

Murder at the Mansion

Body in the Woods

Grave in the Garage

Horror in the Highlands

Killer at the Cult

Fireworks in France

Witches at the Wedding

COLLECTIONS

Books 1-4

Death at the Café

Murder at the Mansion

Body in the Woods

Grave in the Garage

Books 5-7

Horror in the Highlands

Killer at the Cult

Fireworks in France

ALSO BY ALISON GOLDEN

FEATURING INSPECTOR DAVID GRAHAM

The Case of the Screaming Beauty

The Case of the Hidden Flame

The Case of the Fallen Hero

The Case of the Broken Doll

The Case of the Missing Letter

The Case of the Pretty Lady

The Case of the Forsaken Child

The Case of Sampson's Leap

The Case of the Uncommon Witness

FEATURING ROXY REINHARDT

Mardi Gras Madness

New Orleans Nightmare

Louisiana Lies

Cajun Catastrophe

As A. J. Golden

FEATURING DIANA HUNTER

Hunted (Prequel)

Snatched

Stolen

Chopped

Exposed

ABOUT THE AUTHOR

Alison Golden is the *USA Today* bestselling author of the Inspector David Graham mysteries, a traditional British detective series, and two cozy mystery series featuring main characters Reverend Annabelle Dixon and Roxy Reinhardt. As A. J. Golden, she writes the Diana Hunter thriller series.

Alison was raised in Bedfordshire, England. Her aim is to write stories that are designed to entertain, amuse, and calm. Her approach is to combine creative ideas with excellent writing and edit, edit, edit. Alison's mission is simple: To write excellent books that have readers clamouring for more.

Alison is based in the San Francisco Bay Area with her husband and twin sons. She splits her time between London and San Francisco.

For up-to-date promotions and release dates of upcoming books, sign up for the latest news here: https://alisongolden.com/annabelle.

For more information:
www.alisongolden.com
alison@alisongolden.com

facebook.com/alisongolden.books
twitter.com/alisonjgolden
instagram.com/alisonjgolden

THANK YOU

Thank you for taking the time to read *Witches at the Wedding*. If you enjoyed it, please consider telling your friends or posting a short review. Word of mouth is an author's best friend and very much appreciated.
Thank you,

Printed in Great Britain
by Amazon